MURDER IN THE AIR

An Augusta Peel Mystery Book 2

EMILY ORGAN

Also by Emily Organ

Augusta Peel Series:
Death in Soho
Murder in the Air
The Bloomsbury Murder

Penny Green Series:
Limelight
The Rookery
The Maid's Secret
The Inventor
Curse of the Poppy
The Bermondsey Poisoner
An Unwelcome Guest
Death at the Workhouse
The Gang of St Bride's
Murder in Ratcliffe
The Egyptian Mystery

Churchill & Pemberley Series:
Tragedy at Piddleton Hotel

.

Chapter 1

"Is it dangerous?"

Robert Jeffreys took his time to answer, choosing instead to finish writing an address on a pristine white envelope. He had a large belly and tousled grey hair. His fat red cheeks wobbled when he talked, as did the rolls of flesh beneath his chin.

"Is what dangerous?" he responded as he placed his pen in its stand.

"The airship." Arthur Thompson marvelled at the sight of them whenever the light aircraft flew over London; enormous, tubular balloons gliding effortlessly in the air. However, the high whirr of their engines sounded too feeble to keep the ships up in the sky. He liked to watch but had never desired to travel in one.

"Airships? Dangerous?" A bellow of laughter erupted from his employer. "Do you think I'd be investing in them if they were dangerous?" He picked up a delicate cup from his desk and drained it of coffee before plonking it back down onto its saucer. "Have all the biscuits gone?"

"Yes, sir."

"Airships dangerous!" Robert shook his head slowly in amusement. "I don't want to hear any of that kind of talk within earshot of my guests on Friday."

"It's just that I remember there was a crash—"

"Motor cars crash every day, Thompson! Does that mean we should refuse to travel in them? Of course not! What sort of fool do you think I'd be to invite a group of people to travel in something unsafe?" He laughed again. "The trouble with you, Thompson, is that you're a coward."

The insult felt like a punch to the young man's ribs. He balled his fists beneath Robert's enormous mahogany desk and took a deep breath. "Forgive me, sir, but I don't consider myself to be a coward. I'm just a little nervous, that's all. I've never travelled by airship before."

"Few people have! But that's all about to change. Indeed, that's the very purpose of our flight on Friday, is it not?"

Arthur nodded.

"I hope you're not about to go all timid on me, Thompson. I don't want my guests taking one look at your pasty face and deciding they're scared of airships, too. Can I rely on you to make them feel happy and reassured on the day?"

"Yes, sir. Absolutely."

Coward. Arthur had hoped he wouldn't still be hearing that insult at the age of twenty-five, but it was a word that seemed to follow him around. It reminded him of his father.

Robert began to write the address on another envelope. When it came to personal letters, he liked to write everything himself.

Arthur glanced around the room and reminded himself of his exclusive surroundings. His feet were resting

2

on a thick, expensive rug, and the furniture was large and well-polished. Red-and-gold wallpaper matched the heavy brocade curtains hanging from shiny brass poles ten feet above the floor. The tall windows looked out over White-hall and its government buildings.

If Arthur were to lean out of the window, a turn to his right would have afforded him a view of Trafalgar Square, while a turn to the left would have revealed the Houses of Parliament. He had done well for a boy from Watford with a run-of-the-mill education. Sometimes he felt the need to pinch himself as a reminder that he worked for someone so important and well-connected as Mr Jeffreys. For the first time in his life, Arthur's father was proud of him.

But then Arthur thought about the airship again and felt sick. He had heard stories of them falling out of the sky during the war. Apparently, they could break up and burst into flames for seemingly no reason at all.

He caught his breath and wiped the sweat from his palms. There was no getting out of it; he was Mr Jeffreys's assistant. His employer had been interested in commercial airship travel for some time, so Arthur knew it was inevitable that he would have to travel in one before long.

I have to stop being a coward.

Arthur regarded his employer; so large, so wealthy and so fearless. Mr Jeffreys didn't have to worry about travelling in airships. In fact, he didn't seem to worry about anything at all. Sometimes his words stung. *If only he could be a little kinder*, Arthur mused, wondering what he could do to make his boss treat him a little better.

"There." Robert pushed the pile of envelopes across the desk to him. "Make sure these go in the next post."

"Yes, sir."

Robert paused from his work to fight off a coughing fit; something that had been happening so regularly of late.

"Would you like some water, sir?"

His employer dismissed the offer with a wave of his hand. He eventually recovered, though it left his face even redder than before. He wiped his mouth with his handkerchief. "Eleven-fifteen is our departure time from Liverpool Street on Thursday, is it not?"

"That's right, sir."

"We'll be heading to some backwater in the middle of Norfolk. What's it called again?"

"Diss."

"That's the one. I recalled that it had a strange-sounding, rustic name. Now, get those letters posted, Thompson, and then I'll need you to make some coffee for my next meeting. Mr Ketteridge is visiting. He tells me he's found an anomaly in the accounts."

"What sort of anomaly?" Arthur's mouth felt dry.

"I don't know yet. He's probably making more of it than is strictly necessary, but that's accountants for you. It's rather odd all the same. Why are you gawping at me like that?"

"Sorry, sir. I didn't realise I was." Arthur grabbed the letters and rose to his feet.

"Are you alright, Thompson?"

"I'm fine, sir. There's just rather a lot to do. I'd better get on."

"Still worried about the airship, eh?" Robert laughed again. "It'll make a man of you yet. Mark my words, once you've seen the earth from several thousand feet up in the sky, you won't ever look at anything the same way again."

"No, I don't suppose I shall."

Arthur walked over to the door, his legs feeling unusually weak. He attempted to move as nonchalantly as possible but felt there was a strong possibility he wasn't fooling Mr Jeffreys one bit.

Chapter 2

AUGUSTA PEEL ADJUSTED the angle of her light so that it shone more directly onto the copy of *Jane Eyre* she had clamped in the vice. Brandishing her needle, she began to stitch two sections of the book together. A tube train rumbled beneath her feet, and the basement was filled with the noise before it gradually subsided again. The window high in the wall revealed it to be a sunny day, though Augusta hadn't been outside yet.

Tutting, she adjusted the angle of the light again. It didn't seem as bright as usual. *Surely my eyesight isn't fading?* she silently queried.

Augusta stood back from her work and blinked, her eyes sore with concentration. Looking around her dingy workshop, she wished it had a few more windows. She pictured a brighter workshop with plenty of natural daylight by which to work.

A knock at the door disturbed her thoughts.

"Come in!"

The door swung open and a man of about six feet in height entered, wearing a trench coat over a smart suit, and leaning on a walking stick. He paused to remove his hat.

"Detective Inspector Fisher!"

The pair had worked together in Belgium during the war and had recently become reacquainted.

"Philip, please." He closed the door behind him. "It's dark in here, isn't it? My eyes need time to adjust from the bright sunlight."

"I'm over here."

"Yes, I can see where you are. It's not that bad!" He grinned and walked over to her worktable, placing his hat next to a pot of glue. "Hard at work?"

"Just repairing *Jane Eyre*'s spine."

"Ouch, poor Jane. Are you using that enormous needle on her?"

"It's not *that* large. Have you come to collect your book? I've finished it now."

"That was one of the things I came to see you about. How are you, Augusta?"

"I'm well, thank you. And you?"

"I can't complain."

"Good. The book's upstairs in my flat if you don't mind accompanying me up there?" She glanced at the detective's stick. Climbing flights of stairs was no doubt hard work for him.

"Of course. And I'll be able to see you properly that way!"

Augusta led the way out of the basement and they climbed the narrow staircase past the tailor's shop on the ground floor. Augusta lived on the second floor, above the flat where the tailor and his family lived.

"How's Sparky doing?" asked Philip, walking over to the canary's elaborate cage.

"He's very well, thank you, and singing a good deal more now."

"Excellent. I expect you'll be sad to hand him back to Lady Hereford. Is she still in hospital?"

"Yes, and there's no word yet as to when she'll be out. I'm quite happy to look after Sparky for the time being. I had no idea that little birds could be such good companions."

"Animals are remarkable, aren't they? My dachshund, Herbert, is wonderful company. Preferable to my wife and son, some days!" He pulled a face. "Oops, you didn't hear me say that."

Augusta laughed. She pulled a book out of her bookshelf. "Here it is."

"That's it? It looks brand new!"

The book was bound in red cloth with the silhouettes of five children on the cover. *The Adventures of Huckleberry Finn* was written across it in gold lettering.

"It was fairly straightforward to repair. Just a little bit of wear and tear."

He took the book from her. "It had endured rather a lot of wear and tear, I'm afraid. I wasn't particularly kind to this book when I was a boy."

"I think it's forgiven you."

"I'm sure it has now that it's been repaired so well. Thank you."

"Can I offer you a drink?"

"No, thanks. I can't stay long, but I've a favour to ask."

"What sort of favour?"

"Let's sit down for a moment."

Augusta didn't feel sure about taking on another of Philip's 'favours'. She had only agreed to help with Jean

EMILY ORGAN

Taylor's case because she'd happened to be close to the murder scene when the poor woman was killed. Augusta was happy to just continue repairing *Jane Eyre* and think about a new workshop for the time being. Nevertheless, she made herself comfortable in her armchair while Philip perched on the settee.

"It's something Special Branch have been working on," he began.

"Sounds intriguing."

"It'll only take a day. In fact, it may even be less than that."

"Why will it only take a day?"

"Ever been on an airship before?"

"No, I haven't. That's not what you're expecting me to do, is it?"

"Just for a few hours."

"Oh, but I can't, Philip. I hate heights! I couldn't bear to be way up in the sky like that."

"You've flown in a plane before."

"Yes, but that was different. It was during the war. Somehow I was more fearless back then."

"It's just as well you were. But you'd be doing us an enormous service if you agreed to take this job on."

"I don't even understand what it involves. Why would I need to go up in an airship?"

"Special Branch have been conducting surveillance on someone for some time now. Mr Robert Jeffreys, his name is. Ever heard of the chap?"

"No."

"He's filthy rich, apparently, and busy investing in commercial airship travel. I'd say that he probably has a fair bit of competition from the Americans and the Germans, but he doesn't seem to be allowing that to dissuade him. He's had a wartime airship refitted and is taking a group of people for a short flight on Friday. It's a press trip. I can only assume he wants a few decent reports published in the newspapers."

"In which case, most of the people on the airship will be journalists, will they?"

"Yes, I imagine so. But Special Branch would like to know exactly who has been invited, as there may be a dodgy associate or two among them. They're a bit stuck because they can't get their man on board the airship to appraise the guests and watch Jeffreys. Or *any* man, for that matter. They need a woman. There will be waitresses on the airship, you see, supplied by Mrs Perry's Catering Agency. One of whom is about to fall ill with food poisoning."

"Poor girl."

"Not *real* food poisoning! Apparently, Special Branch intend to pay her a little visit to persuade her to feign illness and recommend a reliable friend to Mrs Perry to take her place. This reliable friend will be called Susan Harris."

"That's who I'd need to pretend to be, is it?"

"Yes. Special Branch came up with the name. The papers have already been prepared."

"Papers?"

"Special Branch get very enthusiastic about this sort of thing. I've no idea if they're required, but there's nothing they enjoy more than drawing up false papers. I think you'd acquit yourself extremely well in a task like this, Augusta. I happen to know from our time in Belgium that you're extremely good at surveillance."

"Yes, but I had my feet firmly on the ground there. I wasn't floating about in a giant balloon in the sky."

"I imagine it would be quite exciting to travel in a dirigible."

"It sounds rather funny when you call it that. Rather like a disease."

"I've a bad case of the dirigibles, you might say!"

"Exactly." She sighed. "If I refuse to undertake this task, Special Branch will presumably have to find another woman willing to play the role of Susan Harris."

"I should think so. You're not going to refuse, though, are you? It sounds like rather a lot of fun."

"To you, maybe." Augusta got to her feet. "My under-cover days are behind me now, Philip. I don't want to involve myself in that sort of lifestyle again."

"It would only be for a few hours, Augusta! As soon as Jeffreys is back on the ground, Special Branch will take over again."

"Can't they stop watching him for just a few hours?"

"No. Apparently, they're very close to arresting the man."

"What is it he's done wrong?"

"The word is, he's been acting as an intermediary between the Liberal Party and a number of wealthy indi-viduals in order to sell honours."

"Do you mean to say that an individual can pay to become a lord these days?"

"Apparently so. I've been told that the Liberals need to raise funds for the next election, and they're hoping to build their coffers by bestowing honourable titles upon those who make large donations."

"That sounds terribly corrupt."

"It is corrupt, and you didn't hear it from me. Offi-cially, it doesn't happen, of course, but the reality appears to be a very different story. Perhaps he's invited one or two potential clients onto the airship; I couldn't say for sure. Special Branch want to know exactly who gets on board and whether Jeffreys lets anything untoward slip during the flight."

"And I'm to listen in while serving tea and coffee?"

"Yes, that's about the gist of it."

"But what if I discover nothing useful?"

"Then have no need to worry about it. All you're agreeing to do is keep an eye on him, but as you'll be working as a waitress, it's possible that you won't be able to do so all the time. If you come across anything interesting, you can let me know after the event. Otherwise, just think of it as a chance to enjoy a trip on an airship. I must say that I'm quite envious."

"You could always serve the tea and coffee instead of me."

"I don't think Mrs Perry would have me as one of her waitresses! That's why you're so invaluable, Augusta. Please say you'll do it. Special Branch are offering decent money."

"You should know by now that money is no great incentive for me, Philip, although I suppose it might help me find new premises."

"New premises?"

"Yes. I've decided the basement is a little too small and dark for my liking."

"You've finally realised that! Hasn't everybody else been telling you so for ages?"

"They have, but I don't usually make a habit of listening to other people's opinions. Anyway, I need to find somewhere new to work. I'm rather reluctant to take this job on because I'm quite busy at the moment. I have a lot of books to work on, and I want to look around some new places."

Philip picked up his walking stick and got to his feet. "Well, I've tried persuading you for long enough. If you decide to do it — and there probably isn't much time left to think about it now — feel free to telephone me." He glanced around her flat. "Oh, I forgot. You don't have a telephone, do you?"

Augusta felt a pang of guilt for disappointing him about the special assignment. "Where does the airship take off from?"

"Pulham Air Station. It's somewhere in Norfolk."

"I'd need to travel there by train, in that case."

"Yes."

"Then the job will take longer than a few hours."

"I suppose it would. Does this mean you're agreeing to do it?"

"Yes, I suppose I am."

Philip grinned. "Thank you, Augusta! Special Branch will be delighted. You'll receive a package from them tomorrow morning containing everything you need."

"Good."

"I think you might even enjoy it!"

"Let's wait and see, shall we?"

Chapter 3

As the train whistled and puffed its way out of Liverpool Street station, Augusta realised this was the first time she had left London for more than a year. Despite a flutter of nerves, she was feeling excited about her trip. A change of scene would do her good.

The train picked up speed through the grimy, north-eastern suburbs, and she felt a smile spread across on her face as she was greeted by the green fields and gold, autumnal trees of Essex. It felt refreshing to leave the grey metropolis behind. Augusta had the second-class compartment to herself, so she pulled down the window and let in a noisy gush of fresh air.

Once she had agreed to take on the airship job, preparations had swiftly been made. A large parcel had been delivered to her home containing instructions, falsified personal papers, a waitress's uniform and a dossier on Robert Jeffreys, with a studio photograph of him. She had already read it through but decided to make use of her time on the train to go over it once again. She pulled a large manila envelope out of her bag and slid its contents onto her lap.

Mr Jeffreys was fifty-six and had been married to his wife for almost thirty years. He had five children, all of whom were married with families of their own. The studio photograph had been taken two years previously. He was a large man and his stiff collar appeared to be digging uncomfortably into his fat neck. There was a glint in his eye, which was probably just the effect of the photographer's lights but, coupled with the asymmetrical smile, it gave him a wolfish look. Staring at his face for too long made Augusta feel uncomfortable.

Mr Jeffreys owned four companies: Jeffreys Aviation, Jeffreys Investment Company, Jeffreys Hospitality and Jeffreys and Son, which was a publishing company. Either he lacked the imagination to come up with more inspiring company names or he was a total egotist. Judging by his photograph, Augusta settled on the latter explanation.

Once she was satisfied that she had learned all she could about Mr Jeffreys, Augusta tucked everything back inside the envelope. She looked out at the countryside again and thought about Sparky. She hoped he would cope during her short trip away. She had left detailed instructions with Mrs Whitaker, the tailor's wife, about how to feed him and when to cover his cage for night-time.

Steam billowed past the window and the gentle rock of the train felt strangely comforting. Augusta noticed a plane in the sky and felt a twinge in her stomach as she thought about the airship. The trip would take about eight hours, and they were to fly down to London and circle over the capital a number of times before returning to the air station. It sounded like rather a pointless trip, but Mr Jeffreys was no doubt keen to show off his new toy.

A meal and drinks were to be served during the trip,

and it was the role of Mrs Perry's Catering Agency to ensure that every aspect of the refreshments went smoothly. Augusta had undertaken waitressing work before, so she hoped she would be able to blend in well with the others.

But what if I don't pick up any useful information about Mr Jeffreys? And what if my true identity is found out?

She tried to push these nervous thoughts away, but they kept returning. Having agreed to take on the job, she wanted to do well at it. She wanted Philip to be pleased with her work. *Am I trying to impress him? No, that was a silly thought.* Augusta reassured herself that there was no need for her to impress anyone these days.

Chapter 4

"THERE'S something wonderfully romantic about air travel, don't you agree, darling?"

"What's that?" Edward Somerville looked up from his notebook, irritated by this latest interruption from his wife.

"I remarked that there's something wonderfully romantic about air travel. Up there in the sky with the clouds and the birds…" Jacqueline paused to take a deep breath. "It's so peaceful." She rearranged the emerald-green scarf draped around her shoulders.

They were seated in a first-class compartment on the train to Diss. The plush seats were upholstered in blue velvet and had wide, comfortable armrests.

"You've a reading light there," he said, pointing his pen at the little fringed lantern above his wife's shoulder. "Why don't you read something?"

"Oh, I'm always reading. Sometimes I like to talk. Are you working again, darling?"

"Yes."

"That's a shame." Jacqueline pulled her long, red hair

over one shoulder and began to smooth it. "I like it when we talk."

With her loose hair and flowing dress, she looked like she had just stepped out of a Millais painting. Jacqueline's well-crafted, pre-Raphaelite look was what had first drawn Edward to her. An enigmatic, creative creature who refused to be constrained by modern fashion; that's how she had first appeared. The reality, however, had been far more prosaic, as far as her husband was concerned.

"I've a lot of preparation to do for this article," he responded. "You do realise that my dispatch will be dropped by parachute while we're flying over Croydon Aerodrome, don't you? It'll be printed in the newspaper before we've even landed back in Norfolk."

"How wonderful to think that you can write something in the air and have it published in the newspaper the same day! Your readers will be very entertained."

"I hope so."

"Though it's not like you to write something so frivolous, darling."

"Frivolous? What are you talking about?"

"Well, your writing is usually so terribly serious. With all the reports you write, and what have you, this piece is rather a novelty, wouldn't you say?"

He winced at the suggestion that he would ever write anything light-hearted. "I don't consider this airship flight a novelty at all. It's very important, as we're paving the way for those who will come after us. You do realise that Mr Jeffreys intends to send airships over to America and Africa before this decade is out, do you not?"

"Wouldn't that be wonderful? Travelling by airship to America. Or Africa! I would love that."

"An airship made it across the Atlantic two years ago, so it isn't a new idea. But Mr Jeffreys plans to carry commercial travellers; that's where the difference lies. We're experiencing progress at first hand, and that's very significant indeed. There's nothing frivolous about it."

"I didn't mean to describe it as frivolous, darling. I chose the wrong word. Maybe I just meant that this trip is a little more exciting than the things you usually write about."

"More exciting, yes. But the subjects I write about are always important. How else will the general public find out about the work of the National Unemployed Workers' Movement? One in five men are now unemployed, Jacqueline. Did you hear about that poor chap who died in the dole queue last week?"

"No, I didn't. How awful!"

"And did you know that a baby born in Whitechapel is twice as likely to die as a baby born in Hampstead?"

"No! Oh, I can't bear to think of such a thing!"

"With this pen and paper alone, I can communicate the poverty and inequality of our society to the masses."

"It's very clever of you, darling."

"It's not *clever*. It's *necessary*."

"I still think it's clever."

Edward felt an itch of impatience in his chest. It frustrated him that his wife seemed unable to grasp the severity of the issues closest to his heart.

"I want to write a poem," she said. "In fact, I'd like to compose one while we're in the air. How many poets can say they've done that?"

"I've never met one yet."

"Exactly! That's why I mustn't pass up the opportunity. And once I've found a publisher who's interested in my work, I'm sure they'll be delighted to read a poem that was written up among the clouds. I could write the address as 'somewhere above Norfolk' and follow it with, 'I'm writing to you while floating a thousand feet high in the air.'" She laughed. "Do you think that might catch a publisher's eye?"

"As I've said before, the right publisher will come along at the right time."

"I realise that, but it's taking a dreadfully long time. I do wish you would put in a few good words with your publisher friends, darling."

"I already have, Jacqueline. Now, can you please let me concentrate on my work? I've such a lot to do."

Edward bent over his notebook again. It was important that he got the dispatch just right. With a bit of luck, his editor would publish it in a prominent position. It might even make page two or three. He just had to hope that Jacqueline would stop bothering him long enough to write something worth publishing.

Chapter 5

THE GUESTHOUSE in Diss was simple but comfortable. Once she had been shown into her little room, Augusta placed her trunk on the bed and took out the waitress's uniform. She hadn't had time to try it on before she left London. *What if it doesn't fit?*

The uniform consisted of a plain navy blue dress, a white apron and a white cap. Augusta changed into it and pinned the cap to her auburn hair, then surveyed herself in the cracked mirror beside the wardrobe. Everything somehow fitted perfectly, even though she hadn't told Philip her size. His observation skills were clearly still faultless.

Having committed Robert Jeffreys's details to memory, Augusta carefully burned the manila envelope and its contents over the wastepaper bin. From this moment on, she was Susan Harris from Mrs Perry's Catering Agency.

. . .

Augusta shivered as she waited outside the guesthouse at seven the following morning. The air felt cool and the sky had a pale-blue glow in the east as sunrise approached.

Her stomach felt knotted. *What will the day bring?*

The sound of the approaching charabanc disturbed the peace. When the long, open-topped vehicle stopped in front of her, she saw about a dozen women inside, perched on rows of wooden benches.

The driver hopped down and pulled a piece of paper out of his pocket. "Susan Harris?"

She nodded.

He opened one of the doors for her. "Jump in. You'll have to sit with your trunk on your lap."

"You Molly's replacement?" shouted the young woman next to her, struggling to make herself heard above the noise of the engine. Her black hair was pinned neatly beneath her white cap and she had a wide face and a dark complexion. "I'm Beryl," she added.

"I'm Susan. Have you ever been on an airship before?"

"No, never. I ain't looking forward to climbing the ladder, neither. They say it's really 'igh!"

"There's a ladder?" Augusta gulped.

"Yeah. We gotta climb up the moorin' mast!"

Augusta had assumed the airship would be resting on the ground. She hadn't worked out how it would do so, however, and she felt foolish for not having given the logistics more thought. *A ladder?* She hated heights.

The charabanc bounced along the quiet lanes as the sun's early rays bathed the flat landscape.

Excited chatter broke out as the air station loomed into view. Augusta's heart flipped when she saw the long, shiny balloon with its nose tethered to a mast. It looked out of place nestled in the middle of the countryside. Part of her wanted to travel on the airship, while another part wanted to run straight back to London.

They turned into the road that led to the air station. Aside from the airship, the airfield was dominated by two enormous hangars. There was something almost other-worldly about the place.

Prim Mrs Perry brought Augusta firmly back to earth once the charabanc pulled up next to one of the hangars. She had the bearing of a schoolmistress with her dark woollen dress and a pair of spectacles perched on top of her pinned-up grey hair.

"Hurry along!" she called to her staff as they clambered out of the vehicle.

Most of Augusta's colleagues were young, but she spotted a few who were also in their thirties. One or two looked older still. Mrs Perry spoke to them all as though they were schoolgirls, urging them to gather around and listen carefully to her instructions.

Augusta couldn't stop glancing over at the giant airship. She had seen a good number before, but never at such close quarters. *Is it really airworthy?* She had heard of airship accidents taking place.

"Miss Harris!"

Augusta started and turned back to face Mrs Perry.

"You aren't listening!"

"I am, Mrs Perry."

"What did I just say?"

"The china cups must not be left to air dry. They must be dried immediately with a tea towel."

"And if the tea towel is wet?"

"It must be placed in the laundry bag and a fresh one used instead."

Mrs Perry sniffed, miffed that she had been unable to catch Augusta out.

Once the briefing was over, they placed their luggage in a storeroom, and a man wearing a blue Royal Air Force uniform escorted them over to the mooring mast.

"We're gettin' on a Pulham Pig!" said Beryl.

"Pulham Pig?"

"That's what the locals call 'em."

"Why pig?"

"I dunno." Beryl shrugged her shoulders and grinned.

Some of the women chatted excitedly as they approached the tall, iron mooring mast, no doubt trying to hide their nerves. Augusta didn't like the look of the mast with the narrow staircase winding its way up the centre.

Does it have handrails? How easy would it be to fall through a gap?

Mrs Perry drew up alongside her. "I realise you're a latecomer to the team, Miss Harris, but I expect good work from you today."

"Of course, Mrs Perry."

"I was impressed by your excellent reference from Lyons' Corner House. Seven years at their Leicester Square branch, eh?"

"That's right."

"Well done. You must know Sheila Harding."

"Reasonably well," Augusta lied. *Why didn't Special Branch choose a less well-known establishment?*

"Do give her my regards when you see her next."

"I will."

Augusta stared up at the great belly of the airship and wondered whether she would ever see anyone again, let alone Sheila Harding.

"The ladder's one hundred feet high, but there's nothing to it," said the RAF man at the foot of the mast. "Just keep climbing and don't look down!" He gave the smug laugh of a man who habitually shinned up and down it without fear.

The women approached the narrow stairway in an orderly fashion, and within moments Augusta was disappointed to discover that it was her turn.

She glanced up at the airship again, not liking the way it was bobbing slightly in the breeze. *What happens if the wind picks up? And why does the passenger cabin beneath it look so small and feeble?*

"Up you go, miss," said the RAF man. "Don't go holding everyone up, now."

Augusta glared at him and gripped the cold metal handrails. The steps were of gridded iron, and there was an unwelcome amount of daylight shining through between them. She took a deep breath and began to climb.

"I can't do it!" came Beryl's voice from behind her.

She turned to see her new colleague's crumpled, upturned face beneath her. "I know it looks scary, Beryl, but we're surrounded by an iron frame. We can't fall off." Augusta wasn't sure whether this was true or not, but it sounded vaguely reassuring.

"I hones'ly can't!" said Beryl.

"If *I* can, *you* can. What will Mrs Perry say if we don't?"

This was enough to persuade Beryl to follow in Augusta's footsteps.

Augusta's head was swimming, but she tried to ignore her fear and adopted a steady climbing rhythm, carefully placing one foot in front of the other and gripping the handrail as she made her ascent. The small platforms between the staircases were the most difficult parts because the brief pause provided the temptation to look down. She felt a strong urge to stop climbing and curl up into a ball.

"How are you doing, Beryl?" she asked as cheerily as possible.

"I can't go no 'igher!"

"Just pretend we're not high up. That's what I'm doing." But talking about the height made Augusta's knees feel wobbly. Her head felt as though it were drifting away into the clouds and her feet felt clumsy, as if they might miss a step. Nausea swam in her stomach.

I can't do this.

She stopped at the next platform and crouched down on all fours. Although the position looked ridiculous, it made her feel a little better.

"You alright, Susan?" asked Beryl, pausing behind her.

"I just need a little rest." Augusta had no idea how high up she was, but she knew that it was too high. She tried to slow her breathing, her heart pounding away.

She wanted to get off the staircase but she couldn't go down it because there were people behind her. Augusta closed her eyes and tried to imagine she was somewhere else.

"Just pretend we ain't 'igh up," said Beryl. "That's what you told me."

"Yes, and it was good advice."

"Then pay it some 'eed! There ain't much further to go now."

Augusta groaned and propelled herself up toward the next set of steps. She accidentally glanced down through a gap and saw the tarmac and green of the airfield far below her.

Her stomach lurched. She was frozen to the spot.

"I can't do this, Beryl!"

"Yeah, you can. If *I* can, *you* can. I'm just repeatin' what you told me, 'cause it works!"

"If you say so. Right, I'll try again."

"We're nearly there."

Augusta decided she had to carry on for Beryl's sake. The young woman had overcome her own fear to help Augusta face hers.

She slowly stood to her feet and began ascending the next staircase. Augusta had never climbed anything so high before, and she never planned to again. She concentrated on taking deep breaths and thought of all the curse words she would hurl at Philip Fisher the next time she saw him.

Chapter 6

THERE WAS a cold breeze on the platform at the top of the mooring mast. Although Augusta felt sure there was a wonderful view from up there, she refused to look at it. Instead, she concentrated on the narrow gangplank that led into the nose of the airship.

Encouraged by the RAF man on the platform, the woman ahead of Augusta crossed the gangplank and stepped inside. It was as though she had been swallowed up by a giant balloon.

"You've done the difficult bit now," the RAF man said to Augusta. "Just keep your eyes straight ahead, and in you go."

Augusta held her breath and moved swiftly across the gangplank, staring at the airship's dark interior all the while. She was almost there.

A few moments later, she was inside. She stopped holding her breath and turned to watch Beryl cross the gangplank.

"We did it!" Beryl said with a laugh as soon as she was

by Augusta's side, giving her an unexpected hug. "We're inside the airship!"

"Thank goodness." Augusta was beginning to feel a little more like her normal self. "Let's get on."

They proceeded along a narrow wooden walkway, which was sparsely lit with dim, yellow lights. There were metal girders above their heads and tanks on either side of them. *For fuel, perhaps*, Augusta mused. *Or maybe water.* She wasn't sure. She followed the woman in front until they reached a door. Beyond it, a small flight of steps led down to another door. This one opened out into the passenger cabin.

Augusta was surprised at how beautifully furnished it was. They were standing in a lounge area with large windows on one side. The carpet was pale blue, and colourful landscape scenes had been painted on the walls. Several dining tables had been arranged in the centre of the room, each covered with a white tablecloth and surrounded by dining chairs. Cushioned easy chairs had been positioned beside the windows so the passengers could relax and enjoy the view. It was a room designed for comfort and relaxation, and Augusta immediately liked it.

Mrs Perry arrived a few moments later, but the climb up the mooring mast had left her looking a little less prim than before. She smoothed a section of loose hair back into place and quickly began her next briefing.

"As you can see, this is the passenger lounge. This is where you'll be serving the food and drinks. You'll soon discover that the furniture on board is extremely light-weight. The chairs and tables have aluminium frames because everything needs to be as light as possible. Isn't that remarkable? Let me show you the galley."

A doorway over on the far side of the lounge led into a long, narrow kitchen. Five men in white caps and jackets were lounging beside a table but hurriedly busied themselves as soon as Mrs Perry entered. She gave her waitresses a quick tour of the tea and coffee-making facilities, then showed them where the cutlery and crockery were kept. The instructions were of no great interest to Augusta, but she did her best to pay attention.

When she had finished, Mrs Perry took them back into the lounge and through another door, which led to a couple of bathrooms and several sleeping compartments. Augusta was surprised to find sleeping accommodation there but reasoned that it would be needed for long commercial journeys in the future. The compartments did not appear to offer a great deal of privacy, as they were partitioned only by thick canvas, with curtains in place of doors.

"Very comfortable, wouldn't you agree?" said Mrs Perry, gesturing to one of the beds. "Having said that, I do not want to come in here and catch anyone snatching forty winks!"

The guests arrived in the passenger lounge a short while later. Augusta noted that there were about twenty in total. Most were men in dark suits, presumably journalists from Fleet Street. *Is it possible that one of them is one of Mr Jeffreys's shady clients?*

Augusta watched them closely as she stood with the other waitresses along one wall, but no one looked particularly suspicious just yet. There were a few ladies present; one a blaze of colour with long red hair and a flowing, peach-coloured dress. Another was so fashionably dressed that she wouldn't have looked out of place on the pages of *Tatler* magazine. It amused Augusta that the men could look so dour while the ladies appeared so colourful.

Robert Jeffreys positioned himself in the centre of the lounge and addressed his guests in a loud, pompous voice. An expensive navy-check tweed suit had been stretched over his large frame, and light glimmered on the gold of his rings, tiepin and watch chain.

By his side stood a young man in a grey suit with thin, mousy hair. A smile was fixed on his face, and his down-turned eyes darted around the room while Mr Jeffreys spoke.

Mr Jeffreys introduced the airship's captain, Captain Grainger, in the course of his speech. The RAF officer shifted uncomfortably and looked as though he would rather be tucked away in the control cabin.

Once Captain Grainger had escaped back to his duties, Mr Jeffreys's tone became more rousing. "What we have opening up before us now, my friends, is a new age!" he enthused. "A new age of commercial air travel. We have already seen what aeroplanes and airships can do; the Atlantic has been crossed by both entities now. But no longer is this the sole preserve of inventors, pioneers and the military. We are now approaching a time when ordinary men and women will be able to travel all over the world on these incredible crafts. What better way to see the world than by air?"

He pointed toward the large windows that ran along the side of the lounge. "During your time on board today, please ensure that you look out of the window! You will be admiring a view that very few people have ever seen. And you can enjoy it all in great comfort!" He gestured at the lounge around them. "What you have here is luxury on a level previously experienced only at a top hotel or in one's own home. The staff here will wait upon you hand and foot, serving you the best food and drink for the duration of your journey. All you need do is sit back and relax.

Enjoy yourselves! Oh, and write some marvellous words about the experience for your esteemed publications."

He chuckled, and his guests responded with polite laughter.

Then he threw his arms open wide. "Ladies and gentlemen, this is the future of air travel!"

A round of applause followed, then Augusta felt the floor give a jolt. The guests dashed over to the windows and delighted exclamations broke out as the airship lifted away from the mooring mast.

Beryl gave Augusta a nervous grimace. "We're flyin'!" she whispered.

The airship began to rock a little from side to side, as though it were a ship at sea.

Mrs Perry snapped her fingers at her staff, and the waitresses filed into the galley to prepare the tea and coffee.

"Do you think it'll stop swaying eventually?" Augusta asked Beryl as she filled her coffee pot.

"I 'ope not. I quite like it!"

"I'd prefer it if I happened to be lying down in one of those cabins Mrs Perry showed us."

Augusta was allocated to table three, which was playing host to the lady with the red hair and peach dress, along with a man who Augusta surmised was her husband. He had neat, greying hair, a heavy brow, and dark, brooding eyes. Three other men were also seated at the table.

"Shame we can't smoke on board," commented one.

"Probably something to do with the enormous hydrogen-filled balloon above our heads," replied another.

The two men laughed.

To Augusta's disappointment, Mr Jeffreys wasn't seated

at table three. In fact, he was seated at a table over on the far side of the lounge. It would be difficult for her to listen in on his conversations from such a distance.

"Would you like milk and sugar?" she asked the man with the dark, brooding eyes, who was writing in his notebook. "No milk, two sugars," he responded without looking up.

His wife caught Augusta's eye and smiled, as if silently apologising for her husband's brusqueness.

After serving the tea and coffee, Augusta realised she could get closer to Mr Jeffreys by taking a long detour around the tables and pausing to tidy away used cups and saucers. The tactic didn't work for long, however.

"What are you doing over here, Miss Harris?" asked Mrs Perry. "You're supposed to be on table three."

"I was just helping to clear away some of the dirty cups, Mrs Perry."

"You need only see to the cups on your own table, Miss Harris. There's no need for you to worry about any of the other tables."

"Of course, madam."

Augusta sighed as she returned to her allotted table. Her task would be nigh on impossible to carry out.

Chapter 7

JACQUELINE SOMERVILLE SANK into one of the easy chairs by the window, enraptured by the view. "It's like a patch-work quilt!" she whispered to herself.

Two thousand feet beneath her, the expanse of East Anglia stretched out as far as the eye could see. Hundreds of green and brown fields were edged with woodland or broken up by little grey settlements. Rivers reflected the sky, and she felt sure that she could see the hazy coastline of the North Sea in the distance. Small flurries of cloud were floating almost level with her eyes, and below her a flock of birds was in flight. She longed to be out beyond the window, soaring through the air with them.

She returned to table three, where her husband was still occupied with his notepad. The other men at the table seemed to know each other well and were chatting among themselves. She picked up her pen and notebook, and began the opening lines of a poem. To her delight, it seemed to write itself quite quickly.

When she had finished, she closed her notebook and attempted to make conversation with her husband once again. "You must look out of the window, darling. You won't believe your eyes. It's quite fabulous!"

"I shall go and have a look in a moment. I'm just writing about how we embarked the aircraft. It wasn't for the faint-hearted, was it?"

"Certainly not, but it was more than worth it. I wish we could stay up here all day!" She sipped at her coffee, which had just been refilled by a waitress with auburn hair.

She watched Edward as he worked, his eyebrows knotted over his eyes. His dark-brown whiskers were streaked with grey. He kept his hair short these days and neatly parted to one side. He had worn it longer when they first met, as an act of rebellion against his father. It was such a shame that he preferred to conform these days.

"We simply must look at the view together," she said. "It's an experience that ought to be shared."

"In a moment, Jacqueline."

A few years earlier Edward would have been gazing out of the window in childlike wonder, just as Jacqueline had, but success at the office had made a more serious man of him. She glanced around, wondering if wine or champagne might be served with lunch. A little alcohol usually helped to lift his mood.

"Do you mind if I join you?"

Jacqueline looked up to see a familiar lady in a turquoise three-quarter-length jacket standing beside their table. Bobbed blonde hair peeked out from beneath her blue cloche hat, and she wore several strings of pearls around her neck. Her silk dress, also turquoise, barely reached below her knee. She had high cheekbones and full lips and looked to be about forty-five years of age.

With her dark-rimmed eyes and rouged cheeks, Jacqueline deduced that the woman was trying to look younger than she really was. She had probably once been very beautiful, and to some extent she still was. She brought with her a heady scent, which Jacqueline couldn't quite place. *Lilac, perhaps. Or maybe jasmine.*

To Jacqueline's annoyance, her husband's interest was immediately piqued.

"Of course!" Philip closed his notebook and stood to his feet. "We've met before, haven't we? I can't quite remember where."

Jacqueline suspected he was lying about not remembering the location, as she recalled meeting the attractive woman at a drinks reception a few months previously. She wasn't the sort of lady Edward would easily forget.

"We were probably both reporting on the same event," the woman replied with an Irish lilt. "I'm Miss Daly; Mary Daly. I write for *Aristo* magazine."

"I remember now! Well, in case you need reminding, I'm Edward Somerville. I write for the *Daily Gazette*. This is my wife, Jacqueline. She's a poet."

The dark-rimmed eyes rested on Jacqueline, who felt an uncomfortable twinge. "Not a *published* poet," she felt the need to say. "Not yet, anyway!" She forced a smile and wondered why she always felt it necessary to play down her abilities. When faced with a lady as beautiful and sophisticated as Mary Daly, surely it was better to play to her strengths.

Having always struggled to project herself well, Jacqueline felt a sinking sense of disappointment within her. Confidence seemed to come so naturally for women like Mary Daly.

"You have beautiful hair, Mrs Somerville," Mary said as she sat down.

Jacqueline suspected the *Aristo* reporter had no recollection of meeting her at the drinks reception.

Mary turned to Edward. "Have you seen the view from the window?"

"*I* have," interrupted Jacqueline. "Takes your breath away, doesn't it?"

"It certainly does. About the highest I've ever been is the top of the Eiffel Tower, but this is completely different."

"Do you know Paris well?" asked Edward.

"Yes, I worked there for three years."

Jacqueline felt another wave of inadequacy wash over her.

"I did a year there myself," replied Edward, sitting up and propping an arm across the back of his chair to face Mary more easily. "That was a long time ago now; about twenty years, in fact. I was a correspondent there for a newspaper that has since folded, probably on account of its dreadful missives from Paris!"

He laughed and Miss Daly responded with an amused chuckle.

"How long have you been writing for *Aristo*?" he asked.

"I have a feeling you asked me that the last time we met."

She followed this with a coy smile that Jacqueline didn't like at all.

"Did I? Oh dear. I do apologise." He pulled at his collar awkwardly. "I've met so many attractive Irish society magazine writers that I can't remember what I've asked or what they've told me!"

They both laughed and Jacqueline felt a flush of shame.

Am I just going to sit here while my husband continues his flirtatious conversation with this glamorous writer? She knew it wasn't right, but what was she supposed to do? She couldn't confront them without causing a scene. And the last thing anybody needed in a small room thousands of feet up in the sky was a scene.

"You have an Irish accent," Jacqueline said to Mary.

It was a simple and obvious statement, but it succeeded in drawing the woman's attention away from Jacqueline's husband.

"Yes. I'm from County Donegal originally, but I've lived in England for most of my adult life."

"How interesting that you still have an accent," Jacqueline commented.

"Oh, I wouldn't want to lose it. I'm very proud of my heritage."

"Why did you move to England?"

"There weren't a lot of opportunities back home. It's a shame really, as I miss my family, but London has so much to offer." Miss Daly turned back to Edward. "How long have you worked for the *Daily Gazette*?"

"I'm quite sure you asked me that the last time we met, too."

They both laughed again.

"Too long," he added.

"Oh dear. You're not happy there?"

"I'm currently setting up my own publication with a colleague."

"How exciting! Will it be a daily publication? Or a weekly?"

"Monthly."

"Covering what?"

"The news that people really need to know. I'd say that your average man on the street isn't the least bit interested in the hot air that comes out of parliament. He wants to know about the matters that directly affect him. How he can find a job to feed his wife and children, for example."

"A newspaper for the working man?"

"Yes, that's exactly what it's going to be. About as far removed from a society magazine as it could be."

"There's nothing wrong with a society magazine," replied Mary with a smile. "But I think it sounds like a very worthy cause, Mr Somerville."

"It *is* worthy," agreed Jacqueline. "In fact, it makes you wonder why a man as worthy as my husband would choose to befriend a man like Mr Jeffreys."

"What's that supposed to mean?" responded Edward.

She had his full attention now. "He's rich," she continued, "and doesn't represent the working man at all."

"My friends come from a variety of backgrounds, Jacqueline, and do you know what the advantage of that is? When my new publication is up and running, I'll be able to persuade my wealthy acquaintants, including Mr Jeffreys, to part with a little of their money and put it toward good causes. I can act as the go-between, encouraging richer people to distribute their wealth more generously. A fairer society!" He turned to Mary. "Surely even an *Aristo* writer would agree with that?"

"Oh, absolutely, Mr Somerville."

"How do you know Mr Jeffreys, Miss Daly?" asked Jacqueline. "Is he an acquaintance of yours?"

"No, not at all."

"You've never met him before?"

"Never."

"How did you come to be invited here today?"

Mary shifted in her seat. "The invitation was sent to my editor but she was too busy to attend, so I came in her place. I'm extremely glad that I did. This has been such a wonderful experience."

Mary followed this with a smile which looked unconvincing to Jacqueline.

Chapter 8

Mary Daly wished she could smoke a cigarette and drink an alcoholic beverage. She was sure the invitation had mentioned champagne. *Where is it?* She glanced hopefully at the waitresses, but they were still walking about with their tea and coffee pots.

Mary had heard Robert Jeffreys's name before but hadn't realised exactly who he was until she set foot on the airship. Now she was stuck on board and would have to hope beyond hope that he didn't notice her. There was a possibility he wouldn't recognise her, of course, but what if he did?

Spotting Edward Somerville had provided her with the perfect excuse to stay on the other side of the room. She had hoped that by busying herself in speaking to him she could avoid any direct contact with Mr Jeffreys.

There was only one problem with chatting to Mr Somerville, and that was having to endure the hostile glare of his wife. The woman clearly disliked her, that much was clear. Very few women did like her, in fact, which she considered most unfair. It wasn't her fault that all their husbands were attracted to her.

She stopped a waitress with auburn hair. "Excuse me. Do you know when the champagne will be served?"

"I'm afraid I don't, but I can find out for you."

"Thank you."

"Someone's ready for a drink!" one of the men at the table remarked to his neighbour.

"Aren't you?" she responded.

He seemed embarrassed that she had overheard him. "Well, since you ask… yes. I wouldn't mind one, either."

She flashed him a long smile and enjoyed watching him blush, but her smile quickly faded as she noticed the large form of Robert Jeffreys on the approach. He was accompanied by a young man with shifty eyes, who had been following about at his heels like a pet dog.

"Edward Somerville!" boomed Robert. "What do you think of my airship?"

Edward rose to his feet. "It's very fine indeed, Mr Jeffreys."

"Sit down, please." Robert waved a pudgy hand at him. "Don't stand on my account. *Fine*, you say? Is that all you intend to say in your newspaper report? *Fine?*"

"You know that I shall say wonderful things about the trip, Mr Jeffreys."

"Good! That's exactly what I wanted to hear. The *Daily Gazette* has such a large readership, and I want everyone to be persuaded that this is the very best form of travel. I need them all to start buying tickets as soon as they become available! Although I must say, Mr Somerville, that you're lucky to have been invited on board today."

"Really, sir?"

"Yes. Some of your recent articles have been rather

supportive of the trade unions, which surprises me, given some of the militancy they've been displaying of late."

"I'm not a militant man, Mr Jeffreys."

"That's what I thought. Perhaps you wrote them to appease your editor."

"I do believe in supporting the rights of the common man, however."

"As do I! Just so long as he doesn't get any ideas above his station, eh?" Robert slapped Edward on the back and gave a hearty laugh, which turned into a hacking cough.

"I don't believe you've met my wife Jacqueline before, Mr Jeffreys," said Edward once the coughing fit had subsided.

"No, I don't believe I have." Robert wiped his brow and gave a brief bow. "Welcome aboard, Mrs Somerville."

"Thank you, I'm enjoying the trip very much."

Mary noticed that the auburn-haired waitress was lingering beside the table with a coffee pot in her hand. The society writer had drunk so much coffee that it was practically oozing out of her pores. She wanted to ask the waitress about the champagne again but was forced to bide her time.

"This is my assistant, Arthur Thompson," said Robert, gripping the young man by the shoulder. "My right-hand man."

Arthur responded with a flattered simper.

"Scared stiff he was about coming on this airship!" Robert continued. "You should have seen him yesterday. His face turned as white as a sheet whenever I mentioned the word airship! I thought we'd never get him up that morning mast."

"Quite an experience, that climb," commented Edward.

"That'll soon change, of course," responded Robert.

"It's the way they got used to embarking airships during the war, but as commercial travel takes off we'll find much easier ways to get passengers on board."

"Perhaps the ship could be brought closer to the ground."

"Exactly that."

Mary hoped Edward Somerville would keep the airship owner talking so he wouldn't notice her. Unfortunately, her hopes were in vain and the large businessman's attention soon turned to her.

"I don't believe we've met," he said.

"Miss Daly. *Aristo* magazine."

She met his gaze and gave him a perfunctory smile. And there it was; the unmistakeable glimmer of recognition in his eyes. The only thing that could save her now was the knowledge that he would never dare mention the occasion of their last meeting in polite company.

"*Aristo*, eh? We invited your editor, if I recall correctly." The look of recognition had promptly disappeared and his conduct was suitably formal.

"Yes, Mrs Stapleton. She sent you her apologies, I believe. I was the lucky person who was nominated to attend in her place."

A wide smile pushed Robert's chubby cheeks further apart. "Well, it's an absolute delight to have you on board, Miss Daly." He turned to address the whole table. "We should be passing over London soon. If you've enjoyed the view so far, you won't believe your eyes once we're over the capital. After that, we'll circle over Croydon, just south of London, where your dispatches will be dropped by parachute. And they'll be printed in this evening's newspapers! Isn't that wonderful?"

"I'd better get on with it," said Edward.

"No hurry. We can circle a little longer to allow you

time to finish your dispatch. Doesn't the ride feel smooth? And the gentle rocking motion is rather calming, don't you think?"

"It's an experience like no other, sir," said Arthur.

"You're enjoying it, Thompson! Didn't I say you'd enjoy it? No need for all that melodrama, was there? You'd better get used to it, anyhow. We'll be making a great many more of these trips over the next few years."

"I've written a poem about it," Jacqueline piped up.

Robert raised his eyebrows. "You're a poet, are you, Mrs Somerville?"

"Oh, yes. And I don't believe anybody has ever written a poem on an airship before!" She opened her notebook and ripped out a page, which she handed to him. "Here, Mr Jeffreys. You might like to read it."

"Thank you, I shall have a little look in just a moment. In the meantime, I'd like to inform you all that a delicious meal is being prepared for you as we speak. Until then, be sure to relax and enjoy yourselves. And, above all else, say very nice things in your dispatches about your adventure here today. I must go and speak to the other guests, but I'll be back to chat to you again soon."

Mary breathed a sigh of relief as he walked away.

All I have to do now is avoid him for the rest of the flight.

Chapter 9

AUGUSTA HAD MANAGED to stand in the vicinity of Robert Jeffreys for about ten minutes, but had heard nothing that might be of interest to Philip Fisher or Special Branch. He had then disappeared through the door that led to the bathrooms and cabins, and she had no wish to follow him through there.

The guests had consumed enough tea and coffee, and the fashionable lady seated at her table was after champagne. Augusta made a mental note to ask Mrs Perry about it as soon as she found the chance. In the meantime, she lingered near the table with a coffee pot in her hand as she tried to decide whether any of the guests looked as though they might be the type to purchase honours from Mr Jeffreys.

"What do you think of the airship? Isn't she a beauty?" The voice came from just beside her shoulder and made her jump. She hadn't noticed Robert Jeffreys's assistant approaching her.

"Mr Thompson, isn't it?"

"Yes." He smiled. "How did you know?"

"Mr Jeffreys introduced you at the beginning of his speech."

"So he did. Have you ever worked on one of these things before?"

"No, it's my first time."

"Mine, too. After this I won't want to travel any other way! I suppose it's rather lucky that I'm Mr Jeffreys's assistant. He's planning many more of these trips, you see. Perhaps you'll have the chance to work on board an airship again, too."

"Perhaps."

"We've an interesting bunch here, wouldn't you say? Reporters from a variety of newspapers and a lady from *Aristo* magazine. She's the one in blue." He glanced about him and ran his tongue over his thin lips. "I can't see her at the moment."

"I know who you mean. Miss Daly, isn't it?"

"That's the one."

Augusta wondered whether she might pick up some useful intelligence from Arthur Thompson. "Have you worked for Mr Jeffreys for very long?"

"About a year. I worked as a clerk for a government department before this. It was so boring! Then I answered Mr Jeffreys's advertisement in the *Evening News*. I applied and thought nothing more of it, but before I knew it, he'd taken me on!" He leaned in a little closer. "Between you and me, he doesn't pay very much for such a wealthy man. But it's a wonderful experience working for him. You should see his offices! Right in the centre of Whitehall, they are. That's where it's all happening."

"Is it?" asked Augusta teasingly.

"Yes. That's where all the government departments are. And Downing Street, of course. If you'd told me ten years ago that a young lad like me from Watford would be working in Whitehall, I'd never have believed it. I didn't even do very well at school."

"Why do you think Mr Jeffreys employed you?"

"I work hard, I suppose. I do what I'm told and I seem to do it in a way that he likes. My father always told me I'd be rewarded for my hard work, and he was right."

"It seems to me that you very much enjoy working for Mr Jeffreys."

"Yes, I do. He's quite a personality, and he's achieved a lot, too. Sometimes his remarks can be a bit cutting, but that's just the way he is."

"Is that so? Well, I don't think there can be any excuse for rudeness."

"I didn't say he was rude. He just has a certain manner about him. Perhaps it's to be expected from a man of his generation. He's a product of the Victorian era, you see." He chuckled. "I'm very fortunate, though. He's a very impressive man indeed. Even my father looks up to him, and that's really saying something."

"I see."

"'He doth bestride the narrow world like a colossus, and we petty men walk under his huge legs.'"

Augusta hadn't expected to hear a literary quote from him. "Where's that from?"

"Shakespeare's *Julius Caesar*. Have you seen it?"

"A long time ago, but I can't say that I remember any lines from it."

"It's a wonderful play."

Augusta was keen to return to the subject of Robert Jeffreys. "Did your employer inherit his money or has he earned it all himself?"

"He's earned it all. That's why I admire him so much. The main reason I'm working as his assistant is so I can try to achieve what he has achieved. There's nothing quite like learning from the master, is there?"

Augusta did not feel convinced that this young man had the force of personality to match Robert Jeffreys's achievements, but he already appeared to have had quite a lucky break, so who could tell? He appeared to have money, as, despite having complained about his low salary, he had somehow managed to buy a well-tailored suit.

"I've heard that Mr Jeffreys is friendly with several government ministers," she ventured.

"Oh, yes. He's a donor to the Liberal Party; he won't mind me telling you that. And he counts a number of politicians as friends. With his office only up the road from the Houses of Parliament, it's easy for him to meet with them." He paused and gave Augusta a scrutinising glance. "If you don't mind me saying so, you seem a little different from the typical waitress."

Augusta's heart sank. "What makes you say that?"

"Something about the way you talk. And the fact you knew that Mr Jeffreys has friends in government. How did you know that?"

"Isn't a waitress permitted to know such things?" she asked as calmly as possibly, worried she was letting her cover slip.

"Oh, yes. I think it's a good thing. But the waitresses I've spoken to in the past rarely conversed with me in such a way."

"I like to read the newspapers every day. It's a good way to keep track of what's going on."

"Me too! I think it's extremely important to keep up. I can hardly bear to converse with people who know very little about current affairs."

Augusta decided to play it safe and keep the conversation focused on Arthur. "Well, a man in your position needs to stay abreast of current affairs," she said, "and I'm sure you do an excellent job of it."

"I do. It's no less than Mr Jeffreys would expect of me."

"I can't seem to see your employer at the moment," commented Augusta. "Where has he headed off to?"

"I can't see him either. Maybe he went to use the bathroom. It's quite something, isn't it, using a bathroom while floating way up in the sky?"

"Yes, I suppose it is. It's been very nice talking to you, Mr Thompson, but I should probably get on with my work now. As I understand it, lunch will be served soon."

"Excellent. It's been nice talking to you."

Augusta moved away, unsure what to make of Robert Jeffreys's assistant. He seemed keen to prove himself, but she wasn't sure why.

She moved around the room a little more, then decided to take her coffee pot back to the galley. Just as she was about to pass the door to the cabins, it was flung open and Mary Daly strode out.

Augusta was forced to stop as Mary swept past her. She would have thought it rude if she hadn't noticed the expression on the woman's face.

Mary looked upset.

Chapter 10

THE WAITRESSES WERE CALLED BACK to the galley, where they washed up the cups and saucers, then put everything away. The men in the white jackets and caps were busily preparing lunch. One was carving slices off a large leg of ham, while another tackled a cut of meat that could have been venison or beef.

"It looks as though the guests are to be served cold meat and salad," Augusta whispered to Beryl.

"They was prob'ly 'opin' for somethin' a bit fancier than that!" she replied with a quiet chuckle.

Further down the galley, Mrs Perry was uncorking champagne bottles while two waitresses arranged glasses on circular trays.

Augusta reflected on how well her surveillance had proceeded so far and decided it had been poor. Robert Jeffreys had let nothing untoward slip and Mr Thompson had remarked that she seemed different from the typical waitress. She couldn't risk anyone finding out that she wasn't really Susan Harris. Mr Jeffreys would demand a thorough explanation, and then Special Branch's whole operation would be ruined.

She needed to make a more determined effort to move closer to the airship owner without rousing anyone's suspicions about her true identity.

The door burst open and Robert strode in, startling everyone in the room. "The galley!" he announced to the guests following closely behind him. "Don't mind us," he called out to the staff. "I'm just conducting a tour!"

Augusta and her colleagues squeezed back against the cupboards to make space for the impromptu tour group. A number of reporters were busy scribbling away in their notebooks.

"Here are the people working hard to prepare your lunch," commented Robert. "A cold meal today, but we shall soon be installing ovens on the airships. We're trying to source some that are light enough, as everything on the airship needs to be as light as possible. We can't be doing with any unwanted weight." He patted his large belly and laughed. "Perhaps I should make a note of that myself!"

Champagne was served once the tour had concluded, and the tables were laid for lunch. The next hour was spent serving food and drink, then collecting up and washing plates. Mrs Perry kept a watchful eye on her staff, snapping her fingers and uttering hushed commands to chivvy them along.

"We are now passing over London!" Robert announced halfway through their meal.

He marched over to the windows and his guests joined him. Checking that Mrs Perry wasn't watching, Augusta sidled over and gasped when she saw the great city spread out beneath her.

It was a vast expanse of little grey blocks with the wide, silvery Thames winding its way through the centre. Green parks and squares broke up the grey blocks and church spires, and numerous factory chimneys reached up toward her. The large, grimy dome of Saint Paul's cathedral was the most prominent building of all.

Railway lines snaked in every direction and Augusta spotted trains moving along like little toys. The dockyard was bigger than she had realised. It was lined with bulky warehouses and cranes, and dotted with an array of boats and barges of all sizes.

It was incredible to believe that more than seven million people lived and breathed in that maze of streets below her feet. Somewhere among it all was her flat and basement workshop. Augusta searched hard for Russell Square, but instead spotted Trafalgar Square with the National Gallery on its northern side. Close by sat the buildings of Scotland Yard, where Philip Fisher was no doubt sitting in his office, awaiting her report.

Augusta's shoulders slumped a little. It wouldn't be much of a report.

She felt a nudge in her ribs and turned to see Beryl standing beside her. "Mrs Perry wants us back to work."

While the waitresses finished tidying up after lunch, Captain Grainger returned to the lounge to collect the dispatches that were to be dropped by parachute over Croydon Aerodrome. As he spoke to the guests, Augusta noticed Roberts Jeffreys was once again nowhere to be seen.

"Do you know where Mr Jeffreys has gone?" she whispered to Beryl.

"I 'eard 'e's went for a lie down."

"I wouldn't mind a lie down myself. It was rather an early start, wasn't it?"

"Yeah, I'm tired, an' all. We've only got afternoon tea to serve now and then we'll be done for the day. Only trouble is, we'll 'ave to climb back down that 'orrible moorin' mast again."

Augusta winced. "Oh dear. I'd managed to forget about that for a while. Hopefully, descending it will be easier than coming up."

With Robert Jeffreys missing from the lounge, Augusta had even less chance of keeping a watchful eye on him. *Has he really gone for a lie down? Or has he gone off for a secret conversation with someone?* Augusta decided it would be rather remiss of her not to at least try to find out.

"I need to pay a quick visit to the bathroom," she said to Beryl. "Would you mind letting Mrs Perry know if she asks where I am?"

Beryl nodded and Augusta made her way over to the door that led to the cabins. She slipped through and was met with total silence on the other side.

It felt eerily quiet.

The silence made Augusta more aware of the airship's gentle swaying motion as she slowly made her way past the cabins toward the bathrooms.

A curtain had been pulled across one of the cabins. Presumably Mr Jeffreys was inside it. She paused, holding her breath. No secret conversation seemed to be taking place inside. In fact, she could hear no sound at all. Perhaps the man really was asleep.

It was tempting to gently pull at the edge of the curtain and very carefully peer in. *But what if he isn't asleep after all and he sees me?* She didn't like to think of the trouble that would cause.

Movement up ahead caught her eye, and she saw a

man step out of one of the bathrooms. It was the serious-looking Edward Somerville. Augusta had no choice but to move. She couldn't be seen to be loitering.

She walked on toward the bathrooms and nodded at Edward as they passed each other. He acknowledged her greeting with a brief glance.

Inside the bathroom, Augusta splashed her face with cold water. They would soon be returning to Norfolk, and then her opportunity to help Special Branch would be at an end. It probably didn't matter a great deal that she hadn't obtained any intelligence on Mr Jeffreys, but she felt disappointed all the same. Was it possible that she was beginning to enjoy this brief return to the type of work she had done during the war?

Jacqueline Somerville was approaching the bathrooms as Augusta made her return to the lounge, so there was no opportunity to peek in behind the drawn curtain. There was probably no need to, either; it was only a natural nosiness that had compelled her to do so.

Back in the lounge, Mrs Perry was rounding up her staff and ordering them back to the galley. "You may now have a fifteen-minute break, but you must spend it in there," she said. "Once the clock says twenty minutes to three, you will need to start preparing the afternoon tea."

Inside the galley, the younger men began to act up in the hope of catching the girls' eyes. One stole another's cap while another mocked the pair with bawdy jokes. Their efforts were rewarded with giggles from some of the younger waitresses.

Augusta rolled her eyes, deciding this wasn't much of a break at all, and that she would have preferred to just get on with her work.

A scream from the passenger lounge made everyone freeze.

"What was that?" asked the man whose cap had been stolen.

They all watched the door, half expecting an answer to arrive. They heard raised voices, as though a number of people were talking at the same time.

"Something ain't right," said one of the girls.

"Who's gonna go and find out?" asked one of the men, glancing at his colleagues.

Augusta felt a chill run across her skin.

"I'll go," said Beryl.

"But Mrs Perry said we had to stay in here!" protested one of the older waitresses.

"Somethin's 'appened," said Beryl, walking up to the door. "I'll go an' see."

The door closed behind her and the room fell silent.

The door opened again a moment later, and Beryl reappeared. Her dark complexion had faded to an eerie grey. "It's Mr Jeffreys," she announced in a stunned tone. "'E's dead!"

Chapter 11

SHRIEKS AND GASPS filled the galley. The younger girls huddled together in a group, while Augusta and a few of the others made their way out into the passenger lounge.

Prostrate and sobbing in the centre of the room was Arthur Thompson. Mrs Perry and Jacqueline Somerville were attempting to comfort him.

The guests stood about, their faces pale and their mouths open. The door leading to the cabins was propped open, and Augusta could see a number of people beyond it. She sidled past the small group huddled around Mr Thompson and made her way toward the cabin. She presumed Mr Jeffreys had died while he was taking his rest.

The curtain that had been drawn across earlier had been pulled open. A handful of guests were looking in, one of whom was Mary Daly. Inside the cabin, two uniformed crew members were bending over a bed, upon which the large form of Mr Jeffreys lay face down. Augusta felt a pang of horror as she caught sight of a knife jutting out of his back.

A crew member challenged the onlookers. "You

shouldn't be here unless you have medical training!" he snapped. "Has anyone here ever worked as a doctor or a nurse?"

Augusta and the other guests immediately backed away.

"I'll go and ask," she said, hurrying back to the lounge.

Augusta had assumed from Beryl's announcement that Robert Jeffreys had died a natural death, but there was nothing natural about the knife sticking out of his back. She realised with a shudder that the murderer had to be somewhere on board.

Augusta felt her body quaking as she went about asking the waitresses if they had any nursing experience. As it turned out, one of the older ladies did, though from what Augusta had seen of Mr Jeffreys, he was beyond help.

"I worked on the Western Front for six months," the woman said before solemnly making her way over to the cabin.

Mr Thompson's wails filled the room. "If only I could have done something! Oh, if only!"

"Who found Mr Jeffreys like that?" Augusta asked the reporter standing next to her.

"Mr Thompson," he replied. "That's why he's in such a state, poor chap."

Arthur certainly was in a state. Attempts were being made to haul him to his feet and place him on a chair, and Mrs Perry shouted out for a cup of sweet tea.

"With at least four teaspoonfuls of sugar!" she added.

Captain Grainger appeared in the lounge, but he didn't stay long. Having learned what had happened, he presumably made a swift decision to steer the airship back to Pulham as quickly as possible.

Augusta scanned the room. *Is anybody unaccounted for?* She counted the guests, but they were all present. Whoever had committed the act was standing among them. *But who could it be?*

It was quite astonishing to think that the culprit could be standing there, calmly pretending to be concerned. She stared around at everyone, scrutinising their faces. She received a few suspicious looks in return.

"I can't understand it," said the reporter. "I can't understand it at all. The last I heard, he was having a rest. Someone must have followed him in there and stabbed him in the back. But who? And why? It's completely baffling."

Augusta knew that Scotland Yard would soon be aware of the incident. Captain Grainger would no doubt send out a radio message and the news would travel quickly.

Arthur had successfully been propped up in a chair. Beryl handed Mrs Perry the cup of sweet tea she had requested, and the catering manager tried her best to persuade him to drink it.

"He could do with something a little stronger," said one of the reporters. "How about some brandy? Does anybody have any brandy?"

Augusta thought about Mr Jeffreys's final moments. *Was he aware of what was happening to him? Or was he sound asleep when he was attacked?* It was possible that he hadn't known a thing, as the culprit had clearly attacked him from behind.

They would have to travel back to Norfolk with their grisly cargo. *How will the body be carried down the mooring mast?* Augusta wondered. It was too sickening to even consider.

Philip would have a lot of questions for her when she returned, but her task for the time being was to observe her fellow passengers as closely as possible. If she was lucky, the murderer might let something important slip.

. . .

The descent down the mooring mast wasn't difficult at all. Augusta felt too distracted by the day's events to worry much about it.

There was no breeze in the early autumn evening and the sun was low on the horizon, casting a golden glow across the fields. Augusta felt reassured that every step she took down the ladder brought her closer to the earth.

The guests were already on the ground, having been given priority ahead of the staff and crew. Arthur was finally calm, having been given a cocktail of restoratives.

"Well, that were a trip I'll never forget," said Beryl, shivering. "I ain't gettin' on one of them things again."

"Me neither," agreed Augusta. "Maybe aeroplanes are a better option."

A police constable approached her. "Mrs Peel? You're to come with me."

"Mrs Peel?" Beryl gave her a quizzical look.

Augusta returned it with an apologetic smile. She didn't know what to say.

"Detective Sergeant Turner is waiting for you in the motor car," added the constable.

Beryl's jaw dropped. "They're *arrestin'* you?"

"No, Beryl, please don't worry. I was just helping someone," Augusta said in a fluster. "I'll have to explain another time."

If there ever is another time.

Augusta knew from working undercover in the past that she often made friends only to quickly lose them again.

"I need to fetch my case," she said to the constable as they walked toward the car.

"We've already got it. It's in the trunk of the car."

He gestured at a dark blue Ford Model T, which was parked nearby. A constable sat behind the wheel and a man in plain clothes with fair hair and pale eyes sat in the rear.

When Augusta joined him in the back, he introduced himself as Detective Sergeant Turner. The constable climbed into the front, next to the driver.

"You're to come with us to the police station, Mrs Peel," continued the detective. "We need to know everything that happened on that airship."

"Have you spoken to Detective Inspector Fisher at Scotland Yard?"

"Yes. He knows we're meeting you here."

"And what about the other people on the airship? Everybody on board is a suspect."

"We'll get to them all in good time, Mrs Peel. We already have their names and addresses from the passenger records. Fisher explained why you were on the airship, so I'd like to hear your impressions first."

"How long will it take? I'd really like to get home."

"I'm sure you would, Mrs Peel. The last train for London leaves at half past ten, so we'll drop you at the station in time for then."

As the car pulled away, Augusta looked back at the airship. "How are they going to get Robert Jeffreys off that ship?" she called out over the noise of the engine.

"They'll have to take a window out and lower him down on ropes, apparently."

Chapter 12

"From the sound of things, you had a thoroughly rotten time of it," Philip said as he sat at Augusta's dining table with a cup of tea the following morning.

"Not *thoroughly* rotten. I liked looking out over London. In different circumstances I probably would have enjoyed an airship trip."

"So the key fact we have so far is that Mr Jeffreys went down for an afternoon nap at two o'clock."

"Which I thought rather odd in itself."

"He wasn't in the best of health, apparently, and that was something he was used to doing. His nap was always half an hour long, and it was the custom of his assistant, Arthur Thompson, to wake him at half past two."

"Which was when Mr Thompson found him dead," Augusta said.

"Exactly."

"Arthur Thompson found the body. In which case, he could be the murderer."

"Possibly…" responded Philip. "But why would he want to murder his boss?"

"We don't know the answer to that yet, do we? I had a brief conversation with Mr Thompson, and he told me how grateful he was for his employment with Mr Jeffreys. He alluded to his lowly background and said that he hadn't done particularly well at school. Perhaps he grew up assuming that only men with university degrees would be accepted into the world Mr Jeffreys inhabited. He appeared to be quite excited about working for such an important man. And he enjoyed working in the location of Whitehall, positioned so close to government. He told me his father was very proud of him. The loss of his employer would present a significant loss to him for all these reasons. If he murdered his employer, he would have lost everything he had worked so hard to achieve."

"What were your impressions of the young man?"

"He was keen to impress. He wanted me to think a lot of him, being a lowly waitress, as I was. He even quoted Shakespeare at one point, presumably in an attempt to impose some sort of intellectual superiority."

Philip groaned. "I can't bear it when people quote Shakespeare at me."

"I'm sure you'll meet him in due course."

"Yes, I shall be interviewing him later this morning."

"I can't imagine Special Branch being particularly pleased that the man they were so interested in has been murdered."

"You could say that it's altered the course of their investigation a little. They'll be looking closely at Mr Jeffreys's Westminster connections to see if there's any motive there for having the chap murdered. It could be something to do with this business of selling honours. I've a meeting with the Commissioner this afternoon because Mr Jeffreys was an important man, so there's a lot of interest in this case. My role is to look at all the people who were on that airship and work out which of them could have done it. The sooner I can shake off Detective Sergeant Turner of Norfolk Constabulary the better."

"He wants to be involved, does he?"

"He's claiming the case as his own at the present time! All because the airship happened to take off and land in Norfolk." He shook his head and took a sip of tea.

Augusta sighed. "I didn't pick up any useful intelligence for Special Branch, I'm afraid."

"Rather tricky when your target is murdered, I imagine."

"I passed his cabin while he was asleep. Well, I say that, but he may already have been murdered by then."

"He may well have been."

"I wish now that I'd mustered up enough courage to peek in on him."

"I can quite understand why you didn't. Did you notice anyone else in the vicinity of the cabin while you were there?"

"Two other people. A journalist called Edward Somerville and his wife Jacqueline passed through there at separate times."

Philip wrote this down. "Were they acting suspiciously?"

"No. I encountered them both while they were on their way to the bathroom. You had to pass his cabin to get there."

"They didn't look suspicious in any way?"

"I certainly didn't think so at the time, but I suppose they're as suspicious as anybody else on that airship. It's strange to think that I've already seen the murderer. Spoken to him, even. I watched everyone closely after hearing about Mr Jeffreys's death and felt quite sure that

I'd be able to spot someone looking guilty. People are remarkably good at covering such things up, aren't they?"

"They certainly are."

"It may be difficult to find a motive among the passengers. It's possible that Mr Jeffreys was murdered by someone who was paid to commit the crime. Possibly even a crew member."

"A valid point. We'll be looking into the background of everybody who was on that airship; passengers and crew alike."

Philip drained his cup of tea and sat back in his chair, eyeing her thoughtfully. Augusta had a feeling she knew which question was coming next.

"How do you feel about lending us a hand with this one, Augusta?"

"Haven't I done enough? I thought I was only to be employed for one day."

"That was before someone decided to murder Robert Jeffreys! Your help would be invaluable to us."

"What would you have me do?"

"I don't have any specific ideas just yet, but I'm sure there'll be work to do once I've started interviewing people. You possess various skills that appear to be in short supply at the Yard."

"I doubt that very much."

"It's true, and I think you know it. Will you help?"

"As long as I have enough time to look for new business premises as well."

Detective Inspector Fisher held up his hands. "I promise not to get in the way of your search for new business premises."

"In that case, I'm in."

"Excellent. Shall we begin with getting a telephone installed in your flat?"

"A telephone? Why would I need a telephone?"

He smiled. "Because it's the way forward, Augusta. Once you have a telephone installed you'll wonder how you ever managed without it."

Chapter 13

ARTHUR THOMPSON WAS SEATED in an austere, wood-panelled room in Scotland Yard, every muscle in his body tense. "Am I going to be arrested?" he asked the two police officers sitting opposite him.

One was called Fisher and had entered the room leaning on a walking stick. *What's wrong with his leg?* Arthur wondered. Fisher was the more handsome of the two officers, with dark, greying hair and narrow, wide-set eyes. The pale-faced officer was called Turner, and he was a detective from Norfolk. He had light blue eyes and thick lips, which he frequently pursed in a serious manner.

"We'll decide at the end of the interview whether we're to arrest you or not," said Detective Sergeant Turner threateningly.

The inspector gave his colleague a stern glance, and Detective Sergeant Turner said no more.

Arthur couldn't remember their official titles, but Fisher seemed to be the more senior of the two. And he was from Scotland Yard. *Scotland Yard!* Such a famous name. Arthur could never have imagined that he would one day be sitting within the walls of this famous building. And just around the corner from Mr Jeffreys's office, too! He hoped he'd be free to leave as soon as they had finished with him. The thought of being arrested was absolutely terrifying.

"We need to get as much information from you as possible, Mr Thompson," said Detective Inspector Fisher. "There's no need to be nervous. Just have a sip of that tea and tell us what you can remember about the airship trip."

Arthur felt a little reassured by the inspector's manner. He appeared to be keeping an open mind about the incident, whereas the sergeant was scowling as if he already considered him guilty.

Arthur lifted a trembling hand and reached out for his tea. He tried his hardest not to spill it as he lifted it to his mouth and took a sip. The warmth that followed in his chest made him feel a little better. "Where would you like me to start?" he asked the inspector.

"Anywhere you like."

Arthur liked this response; it wasn't too prescriptive. "Oh, alright. Well, I was rather nervous about the trip, but I enjoyed it in the end. At least, I was enjoying it until the dreadful incident occurred. Mr Jeffreys had been very excited about the excursion. He'd invited journalists to travel with him and write about it in their newspapers. He hoped they'd write nice things. In fact, he told them to! I'm sure they would have done anyway. They all seemed to be enjoying it until... well, you know what happened."

He felt a lump in his throat but tried to continue. "Mr Jeffreys wanted to venture into commercial travel and..." He tailed off again, recalling how excited his employer had been about his plans for the future. None of them would be realised now.

"Do go on," encouraged Detective Inspector Fisher.

"Everything was fine in the beginning," said Arthur, recovering himself. *I have to tell them as much as I possibly can. I have to be helpful.* His hands were shaking a little less now. "Mr Jeffreys gave a welcoming speech, and then we lifted off the mast and he made a point of speaking to everyone on board. We were served tea and coffee, then champagne. After that there was a tour, followed by lunch. It was after lunch that Mr Jeffreys went for a lie-down."

"Which was a common practice of his."

"Yes. He was in the habit of having a lie-down after lunch. He kept a chaise longue in his office to serve as a resting place. He had a little bit of trouble here, you see." Arthur patted his chest.

"Heart? Lungs?"

"Lungs. He was prone to coughing fits. He didn't like to grumble, but he'd seen the doctor about it. He told me it was probably something to do with his age. There was no chaise longue on the airship, of course, so he went into one of the cabins for a lie-down."

Detective Inspector Fisher put on his reading spectacles and wrote this down. "From two until half past, is that right?"

"That's correct."

"And you went in to wake him at half past?" asked Detective Sergeant Turner.

"Yes. That was the time we'd agreed on. In fact, I probably went into the cabin a minute or two beforehand to ensure that he'd be fully awake by half past. Sometimes it took him a while to come round."

"What were you doing while your employer was having his nap?" asked Detective Inspector Fisher.

"I made conversation with the guests. It was very important to Mr Jeffreys that they were enjoying their flight and were happy with everything. Oh, and the captain came into the lounge to collect the reports that were to be dropped by parachute over Croydon Aerodrome."

"I understand that didn't happen in the end," the inspector said.

"No, because we'd found Mr Jeffreys by then, and..."

"His death had been discovered, which meant that all other plans for the trip had understandably gone out of the window, so to speak."

"Exactly."

Arthur felt less shaky now, but his palms were still sweaty. He picked up his cup to take another sip of tea, worried that it was in danger of slipping out of his hands. The police officers were watching him closely as he drank. He didn't like being scrutinised like this. *What clues or hints are they looking for? Are they hoping I'll give something away?*

"Did you see anybody else walk through the door to the cabins while Mr Jeffreys was having his rest?" asked Detective Inspector Fisher.

"Yes, quite a few people."

"Can you recall their names?"

"Mr and Mrs Somerville... Edward Somerville writes for the *Daily Gazette*. Mr Jonathan Faulks... he writes for the *Daily News*. Mr Beresford, I think... I can't recall which paper he writes for. Oh, and one or two of the crew members. Including a waitress, I think."

"Did you notice if anybody happened to be missing while Mr Jeffreys was having his nap?"

"Missing for the entire time, you mean?"

"For any reasonable length of time. Longer than it might take someone to visit the bathroom, for example."

"Well, that's rather subjective." Arthur laughed, but neither police officer shared his joke. "In short, no. No one was conspicuous by their absence, if that's what you mean."

"Tell us what happened when you went to wake Mr Jeffreys, Mr Thompson."

Arthur began to tremble again. "I noticed it was approaching half past two, so I excused myself from the conversation."

"Whom were you talking to?"

"The guests in the lounge."

"But which guests? To whom did you have to make your excuses?"

Arthur scratched at his head as he tried to recall. All the conversations from the previous day had blurred into one. "I can't quite remember. It must have been one of the news reporters. Possibly the chap from the *Evening News*."

"Who was the chap from the *Evening News*?"

Arthur closed his eyes and tried to remember. "Mr Macmillan, I think it was, but I may be mistaken. I know I spoke to him while Mr Jeffreys was having his rest, but I can't be certain that he was the last person I spoke to before I went to wake him."

"Never mind. Then you made your way to Mr Jeffreys's cabin, did you?"

"Yes. The curtain was pulled across, so I pulled it back and then..." The memory of the shocking incident flooded his mind. He covered his face with his hands and leaned over the table.

Oh, it was horrible. So horrible.

"And then what?" asked Detective Sergeant Turner.

"Just give him a moment," Arthur heard Detective Inspector Fisher say.

Arthur removed his hands from his face and slowly sat up. "And then I saw the most terrible sight. He was just lying there with a knife sticking out of his back, as though it had just been stuck into a square of butter! He'd taken his jacket off for his rest, and the knife was there in the middle of his waistcoat. Someone had plunged it right in. I called his name, but there was no reply."

"Just to be clear," said Detective Sergeant Turner. "Can you describe the position in which you found your employer?"

"He was lying face down on the bed. His face was on the pillow."

"What position had he been lying in when you left him in the cabin?"

"I've no idea. He merely went in there and told me to come and wake him in half an hour."

"Did you try to rouse Mr Jeffreys?" asked the inspector.

"I wish I could have, but when I saw that knife… and when I saw how motionless he was…" Arthur's voice cracked and he felt a burning sensation behind his eyes. "I instinctively knew he was dead. I wanted to pull the knife out, but I'd heard before that you shouldn't do such a thing; that it was dangerous. It causes blood loss, doesn't it? I didn't dare do that, but I took hold of his shoulder and shook him a little. Only slightly. As I leaned in over him, I saw that his face was turned to the side and it was just white. Cold and white. His eyes weren't blinking at all.

"I felt for a pulse but there was nothing. I just knew then that somebody had ended his life in one fell swoop. And then a horrible sickness came over me. My legs felt weak and it was all I could do to stagger back out through the door into the lounge to raise the alarm."

Arthur paused, breathing heavily. Perspiration had broken out across his brow.

"That's when I collapsed, and I remember very little after that. I came round quite quickly, apparently, but the shock… I can feel myself shaking again now as I recall it. I couldn't comprehend what had happened. I still can't comprehend it now. I just cannot understand how someone could do such a thing."

"Any ideas as to who might be a suspect?" asked Detective Sergeant Turner.

"We'll move on to that in a moment," said Detective Inspector Fisher. "Let's give the young man a bit of a breather first. Finish your tea, Mr Thompson, and take a moment to compose yourself. We understand this isn't easy to talk about. You've had a dreadful shock, and it's important that you take your time."

"May I have a cigarette?"

"Of course." Detective Inspector Fisher retrieved a packet of cigarettes and a lighter from his jacket pocket and passed them across the table.

"Thank you." Arthur reached out for them. "It's not something I do very often. Just occasionally."

"Completely understandable."

Detective Sergeant Turner also helped himself to a cigarette, but his superior abstained.

The inspector waited for Arthur to take a few puffs on his cigarette, then said, "Tell me about your working relationship with Mr Jeffreys."

"I enjoyed my job very much. I felt fortunate to work for such an important man. It wasn't the sort of thing the men in my family usually did. In fact, no one else did it. My father was extremely proud."

"You worked well with Mr Jeffreys, did you?"

"Yes, very well. He knew he could rely on me, and I learned a great deal from him."

"What sort of a man was he to work for?"

"He had high standards, but I didn't mind that. I was keen to work hard. He didn't even pay a particularly large salary, but I didn't mind that either. It was the experience I was after. I want to be just like him one day and earn the sort of money he did. I was learning so much every day... And now it's… it's all gone."

"Was he ever unkind?"

"No, he wasn't an unkind man. Sometimes he would make a joke or two at my expense, but it was only ever a joke. And it was mainly because I was a good deal younger than he was. But I knew I was invaluable to him, and he relied on me. I looked after all the finer details for him."

"Were you involved in all his affairs?"

"I like to think that I was."

"You dealt with all his correspondence?"

"A good deal of it, but not all. There were some letters he liked to write himself. To personal friends and so on."

"Did you have concerns about any aspects of his work?"

"Concerns? None whatsoever! Why should I have had?"

"No reason. Can I ask if there had been any sort of disagreement between you before his death?"

"None at all. As I say, he used to make the odd joke at my expense, but it was all done in good humour. There was never any serious disagreement between us. We worked well together, even though we were from completely different backgrounds… and different ages, too. It was a good working relationship." The lump returned to Arthur's throat. "I'm going to miss him very much."

Detective Inspector Fisher took off his spectacles and sat back in his chair, as though he were ready to conclude the interview.

Detective Sergeant Turner leaned in closer over the table. "Who do you think did it, Mr Thompson?"

"I have no idea," responded Arthur. He didn't like the way the man's pale eyes were staring into his.

"Did he have any disagreements with anyone that you knew of?"

"None that I knew of, no. But there were a few minor matters that might have led to a dispute."

"Such as?"

"I call them jokes more than anything."

"Can you elaborate?"

"It's difficult to remember them all, as they're so small and don't really matter. But one example would be his annoyance with Mr Somerville."

"What was the reason for that?"

"He didn't like some of the articles Mr Somerville had been writing. Mr Jeffreys thought they were too supportive of the 'militant trade unions', as he described them."

Detective Inspector Fisher nodded. "Not a serious enough dispute to commit murder over, though?"

"Oh, no! They were all very minor indeed."

Detective Sergeant Turner checked his watch.

"Is there anything else you need to know?" Arthur asked. He wanted to show that he could be helpful, desperately hoping that they wouldn't suspect him.

"Not at the moment," replied the inspector, "but I'm sure we'll need to speak to you again at some point."

"Of course, of course." Arthur began to breathe a little more easily. *Is it possible that they're about to let me go?*

"You know where to find me whenever you need me," said the young clerk. "Mr Jeffreys's office is just around the corner from here, and I'll be there for a while, helping his lawyer sort out his affairs." Arthur pulled a handkerchief out of his pocket and wiped his face. "It'll feel very odd without Mr Jeffreys there."

"I'm sure it will," replied Detective Inspector Fisher. "Good luck with it all, Mr Thompson."

"Thank you. Am I free to leave?"

He nodded.

Arthur jumped to his feet before the inspector could change his mind. "Thank you," he said. "Thank you very much indeed."

Chapter 14

"MURDER ON AN AIRSHIP?!" Lady Hereford exclaimed to Augusta, examining the newspaper in her hand.

She was sitting in her hospital bed, propped up by an abundance of pillows. She had neatly waved white hair and wore a ruffled pink bed jacket. Her eyes were a striking blue, and pink circles of rouge had been rubbed onto her cheeks.

Augusta was seated in the chair beside Lady Hereford's bed. The pleasant scent of rose water hung in the air of the light, spacious room at Middlesex Hospital. A large window provided a view over Fitzrovia's rooftops.

Augusta peered at the news report, accompanied by a photograph of the airship tethered to its mooring mast. "Would you believe me if I told you I was there when it happened?"

Lady Hereford rested the newspaper on her lap and smiled. "Have you been involved in something interesting, Augusta?"

Augusta nodded and proceeded to tell Lady Hereford all about the previous day's events.

"Gosh!" said Lady Hereford when her visitor had finished. "Do you know what I would have done? I would have peeked in through that curtain!"

"I was worried he might see me."

"He was probably dead by then, and the murderer might still have been in there. You'd have caught him red-handed!"

"Perhaps, but of course I had no idea that Mr Jeffreys was dead at the time."

"I don't suppose you did. What an adventure, though! How I'd love to have been on that airship. I don't suppose I'll ever get to travel on one now."

"Perhaps you will one day; we'll just have to see. You'll be pleased to hear that Sparky is fine, and that he was well looked after by Mrs Whitaker while I was away."

The old lady's face fell. "I can't imagine he enjoyed that very much."

"Why not?"

"She talks too much. He's never been good with people who talk a lot. He doesn't mind being chatted to, but he also likes his peace and quiet. That's why I chose you to look after him, Augusta."

"There weren't many other people I could have asked," Augusta replied. "Do you really think she would have talked at Sparky a lot?"

"Undoubtedly. You should see her when she comes in here. It's always nice to receive visitors, but she keeps talking to me even after I've nodded off. Doesn't even notice! Sometimes I just pretend to nod off, but she doesn't notice that either."

"Oh dear. Well, it was only for one night, and Sparky doesn't seem to have been too adversely affected. He was singing very happily this morning."

Lady Hereford smiled. "Was he indeed? That's lovely to hear. Shows he's happy. Oh, I do miss him."

"Have you any idea how much longer you'll be in here?"

"A little while yet."

Augusta was wary of asking exactly what was wrong. It seemed a little too personal, and she surmised that Lady Hereford would have volunteered the information if she had felt inclined to share it.

"I can only hope that they'll catch the person who murdered Mr Jeffreys on that airship soon," continued the old lady. "He was quite a rich man, from what I've read. I don't recognise him, so I can only deduce that he's one of those chaps who's had to work for his fortune. I expect the police will want to hear a lot of information from you, Augusta, given that you were there."

"They will. In fact, I've been asked to help out with the investigation."

"Have you indeed?" Lady Hereford's blue eyes grew wider.

"That's between you and me, though. It's not supposed to be common knowledge."

"Of course." Lady Hereford tapped the side of her nose conspiratorially. "Your secret's safe with me, Augusta. Presumably this is to do with that police friend of yours. Who is he, exactly?"

"An inspector at Scotland Yard."

"Married?"

"Yes."

"Shame."

"Why do you say that?"

"No reason, other than that you could do with someone to share your life with."

Augusta spluttered. "Not Philip Fisher!"

"No, clearly not. But from what I know of you, Augusta, you're not exactly the sociable type. You need to get out more if you want to meet someone."

"I don't want to meet anyone."

"Very well. If you say so." Lady Hereford glanced at the door. "That nurse is taking her time with the tea, isn't she? I must say, Augusta, that you're much more exciting than some of my other visitors. Mrs Whitaker... well, we've already discussed her. And sadly Mrs Hardwick has little more to say for herself these days than to bore me senseless about who she's been sitting next to at dinner parties. It's all rather tedious, especially when one has no hope of being invited to a dinner party oneself anytime soon. Once people learn that one is confined to a hospital bed, the invitations swiftly dry up."

"I'm sure the invitations will return once you're fit and well again, Lady Hereford."

"Perhaps. Now, other than encountering murders on airships, what else has been happening?"

"I'm on the lookout for new premises."

"You want to move away from Marchmont Street, do you?"

"I'm very happy with my flat there, but it's the basement that's the problem. It's rather small and dark."

"Isn't that what you'd expect from a basement?"

"It is, and there was a time when I enjoyed it. But sometimes I spend a whole day working down there, and the only sunlight I see are the rays that filter in through the little window."

"You could always go for a walk."

"I often do. Russell Square is very close by, as you know. But I'd like a better workshop with space for a small shop to sell the books I repair."

"That's an excellent idea, and it's about time you

emerged from that basement. I can't say I ever liked the place myself. Have you looked at any other premises?"

"Not yet, and I shan't have a great deal of spare time to do so if I'm to help with the investigation into Mr Jeffreys's murder."

"A good friend of mine has a property available near the British Museum. Do you think that might suit?"

"The location sounds perfect, but I'd need to see it first."

"Of course you'd need to see it! That goes without saying." The old lady reached over to her bedside table and retrieved a pad of notepaper. She picked up a pen, scribbled down a name and address, then tore off the note and handed it to Augusta. "There you go. Write Bertie a letter and ask if you can take a look. And don't forget to mention my name."

Chapter 15

DETECTIVE INSPECTOR FISHER called on Augusta that evening.

"Twice in one day!" she exclaimed. "To what do I owe the pleasure?"

"I hope you feel extremely honoured," he responded with a smile. He stepped into the living area and removed his hat. "Someone will be here in a few days to install your telephone. That'll mean I can telephone you when I need to speak to you rather than wearing out my shoe leather each time. I've said it before, but you'll be surprised how often you use it once it's set up."

"I should think your household is a little busier than mine, Philip."

"I imagine it is, with the wife and son, and not forgetting Herbert the dachshund! The only downside of the telephone is that it makes it easier for the Yard to contact me when I'm off duty."

"Tea, coffee or brandy?"

He checked his watch. "At this hour, I'll say brandy. Thank you, Augusta." He took a seat on the little settee. "I

Murder in the Air

interviewed Arthur Thompson today. I'm not quite sure what to make of him."

Augusta took a bottle and two glasses out of the cupboard. "How did he seem?"

"Very nervous. He was worried we were going to arrest him."

"A valid concern, considering that he's the most obvious suspect at the moment."

"Yes, he is. I was hoping he might give us a little more insight into Mr Jeffreys's business activities, but either the chap is covering for him or he's genuinely ignorant of any wrongdoing. He seems rather young and naive, so I'm tempted to assume the latter. I wondered if it might be useful for you to have a chat with him."

"Really? But I've already had a chat with him."

Augusta handed Philip his drink and sat down.

"That may be, but it would be good to get a little more information out of him. I think he clammed up a bit when we spoke to him because he was so nervous. If he were to bump into a waitress he recognised from the airship, he might be tempted to open up a little more."

"You want me to pretend to be a waitress again?"

"Only for the purposes of speaking to Mr Thompson. I think you might get further with him if he feels like he's talking to someone of a lowlier status."

"*Lowlier status?*"

"Not my opinion, of course, but that's the way he seems to view things. Status matters a great deal to Arthur Thompson."

"So you're the very important Scotland Yard detective and I'm the lowly waitress."

Philip laughed. "Of course not! I'm only talking about the way it appears in Mr Thompson's world. Speaking to a lowly waitress might just change his approach."

"I'm trying exceptionally hard not to be offended here, Phillip."

"I can tell. But you're so very good at this sort of thing."

"I don't know that I am, actually. There was a moment during our conversation on the airship when he noted that I didn't seem like the typical waitress. I let my curiosity get the better of me and asked one too many questions. I'll have to avoid doing that the next time I meet him. How would I go about speaking to him? Would I just casually bump into him in the street?"

"Yes, that should do it. He'll be assisting Mr Jeffreys's solicitor at the office in Whitehall over the next few days. Perhaps you could bump into him somewhere around there."

"Under what pretext?"

"Perhaps you could say that you had recently taken employment at a tearoom or coffee house close by."

"Alright. I'll need to stick with the name I was using before. Susan Harris, wasn't it?"

"Yes. It suits you, Susan." Philip laughed and took a sip of his drink.

"What have you learned so far about the knife used in the murder?" Augusta asked.

"It's a sizeable piece; the blade is about six inches long. We suspect it was taken from the airship galley."

Augusta recalled seeing the men slicing up joints of meat for lunch. "Goodness. The culprit somehow managed to take it without anyone noticing, did he?"

"Yes, and that was no mean feat because it's quite a large knife. Perhaps someone hid it inside a bag they were carrying."

"They may have done. That would narrow it down to the ladies, as they were all carrying handbags. Although a knife of that size might not easily fit inside a handbag. Has it been dusted for fingerprints?"

"Yes, but the culprit appears to have wiped the handle."

"Oh, no. How unfortunate. The murderer must have been calm and composed to remember to do that."

"Yes. Very composed indeed."

"What could the killer have wiped it clean with? A handkerchief perhaps?"

"I imagine so. Or a scarf. The sleeve of a jacket, perhaps. We should be able to narrow down the suspects by establishing exactly who went into the galley."

"I don't think we will."

"Why not?"

"Because *everybody* went into the galley. Mr Jeffreys took the guests on a tour while lunch was being prepared, and they were all shown into the kitchen. I was in there at the time."

Philip sighed. "Wonderful."

"I didn't see anyone pick up a knife while they were in there. I only saw the kitchen staff using knives, much as you'd expect."

"Lunch was being prepared at the time, you say? If food preparation was underway, knives may have been left lying about on the worktops. I think that must have been when our murderer took the weapon."

"Do you think he would have had any bloodstains on his clothes?"

"Normally when someone is stabbed, I would say yes. However, in this case Mr Jeffreys died from a single stab wound to the back. That's what the pathologist has confirmed. There was a good deal of blood, but because the knife was left in Mr Jeffreys's back, and he remained completely immobile after the attack, I think our killer must have got away relatively cleanly."

"Luckily for him. Or her."

"It may well be a *her*." Philip paused to retrieve his notebook from his jacket pocket. He opened it up, squinted inside, then tutted before finding his reading glasses in his other pocket and putting them on. "Miss Mary Daly," he commented. "Do you recall her?"

"The glamorous lady?"

"I wouldn't know. I haven't met her yet."

"Writes for a society magazine, I think."

"Yes, that's the one. My men have been speaking to some of the airship passengers, and several remarked on the fact that her mood altered quite suddenly during the flight."

Augusta recalled how she had seen Miss Daly looking upset as she strode out of the door that led to the cabins.

Was that while Mr Jeffreys was taking his nap? No, it was much earlier.

"I remember now. She was all smiles at the start, but then something must have happened because I saw her looking very serious a little while later."

"Had she had a disagreement with someone?"

"I didn't overhear anything, but I definitely remember her looking unhappy."

"I shall be interviewing her in due course, but I wondered if you might like to have a little chat with her first. Woman to woman. She may be more willing to confide in you than me."

"Woman to woman. Not *waitress* to woman, then?"

"I don't think there's any need for you to pretend to be a waitress with her, is there? While I can imagine Arthur Thompson being more comfortable with someone of a lowlier status, a journalist like Mary Daly is probably confident in speaking with people of all backgrounds. No, your normal self should do well enough."

"That's reassuring. Do you want me to tell her I'm assisting you with the investigation?"

"Perhaps just tell her you're a private detective or something along those lines. It'll be interesting to see what you can get from her." He stood to his feet. "Well, I must head home. My wife's never happy when I've got one of these big investigations going on. She hates eating dinner alone."

"Eating alone isn't that bad!"

Philip regarded Augusta for a moment, as if suddenly regretting his words. "No... I... That's good to hear. I imagine it's not so bad at all. I suppose you're accustomed to it! Foolish of me to say it, really."

"It wasn't foolish if that's how your wife feels."

"Indeed." He put his hat back on. "Goodnight, Augusta, and good luck with Mr Thompson and Miss Daly. Do let me know how you get on."

"I will."

Chapter 16

"HAS HE NOT TURNED UP?" asked the waitress, glancing down at Augusta's empty cup.

"Who?"

The waitress laughed. "I was just having a joke with you. Only, you've been here a while and you keep looking out the window, so I wondered if you were waiting for someone. Would you like another refill?"

Augusta checked her watch. She had been sitting in the cafe on Whitehall for more an hour. "Another cup would do nicely, thank you."

She turned back to the window, where rivulets of raindrops were trickling down the pane. People out on the street were walking briskly past, beneath their umbrellas. Across the road stood the ornate stone building that housed Robert Jeffreys's office.

Surely I'll catch sight of Arthur Thompson soon.

Augusta wasn't sure how much longer she could get away with occupying her seat in the cafe.

Her cup had just been refilled when the man she was waiting for stepped out of the building.

Augusta quickly stood to her feet. "I have to go now, but thank you all the same," she said to the startled waitress. Then she picked up her umbrella, left a sixpence on the table and dashed out of the cafe.

Arthur Thompson was heading in the direction of Westminster, his head bent down against the rain. A gust of wind flapped at his raincoat and threatened to blow his hat off. Augusta waited for a gap in the traffic, then called over to him.

"Mr Thompson!"

He glanced about, seemingly unsure as to who had called his name. She waited for a bus to pass by, then skipped across the puddles in the road to join him.

It took him a moment to recognise her. "I recall your face, but I must apologise. I can't remember..."

"It's quite alright. I don't think you ever knew my name. It's Susan Harris. I was a waitress on the airship."

"Good Lord, yes!" He slapped his forehead, as if admonishing himself. "What a surprise! What are you doing here?"

"I've just been for an interview at a cafe close by."

"What a funny coincidence! Mr Jeffreys's office is just up the road from here. In fact, I think I told you about it. We had a brief conversation on the airship, didn't we?"

"Yes, that's right. You did tell me about an office on Whitehall."

She held out her umbrella and he ducked his head underneath.

"Thank you," he said. "I've mislaid mine."

"How are you faring?" she asked.

"Not very well, to be honest with you. I still can't believe Mr Jeffreys lost his life in such a terrible manner, and to make matters worse I've had the police questioning me."

"I imagine the police are talking to everyone, aren't they?"

"Yes, I suppose so. Have they spoken to you yet?"

"Yes." This wasn't a complete lie.

"Awful, isn't it? I understand that they have to do so in order to find out who murdered poor Mr Jeffreys, but it's just dreadful. Whenever a police officer speaks to me I feel convinced that I've done something wrong, even though I haven't. But I haven't been arrested yet, so perhaps I shall be alright."

He ran his tongue over his lips and Augusta recalled, with mild disgust, that he had done the same thing during their conversation on the airship.

"Have you any idea who might have murdered Mr Jeffreys?" she asked.

"No. No idea at all. I can only hope that someone saw something out of the ordinary. If they're interviewing everyone, they're bound to find someone who saw something suspicious, aren't they? I told the police what I saw, but several people came and went while Mr Jeffreys was having his nap that afternoon. Someone knows something, that's for sure."

"They certainly do. Isn't it awful to think that the guilty party was on the airship with us the whole time?"

Mr Thompson shuddered. "Terrible. A murderer in our midst!"

"Do you think Mr Jeffreys might have upset somebody?"

"That could possibly explain it, but I simply can't think who. Funnily enough, the police asked me the same question, but I really don't know whether he'd had a disagreement with anyone. He never mentioned it to me, and I think he would have if anything significant had happened.

He liked to have a bit of a grumble about people some-times. Perhaps something occurred in his private life and he wanted to keep it quiet."

"Did he tell you much about his private life?"

"I know that he was married and had five children. I never met his wife, but he talked about her in glowing terms. Other than that, his private life was his own business as far as I was concerned. I knew very little about it, and quite rightly so."

"Maybe one of the news reporters did it."

"Maybe so. None of them struck me as a potential murderer, but I suppose that's the problem we face. No one on that airship looked like a murderer, did they? But someone had to have been."

"Yes, exactly. The police have a difficult task ahead of them. What will you do now?"

"I'm helping Mr Jeffreys's solicitor with all the adminis-tration that's required. I really don't know what to do after that. I hope I'll be able to find work as an assistant to someone else. Hopefully I've gained enough experience over the past year to be employable." He glanced about. "It's rather damp out here, isn't it? What do you say we get a drink somewhere a little drier?"

"I have to head home now, Mr Thompson. Perhaps another time."

This would have been the perfect opportunity for Augusta to acquire more intelligence for Philip, but there was something about Mr Thompson that made her feel uncomfortable. Perhaps it was the manner in which his eyes darted around or the way he licked his lips. Or perhaps it was something else altogether. Either way, she decided it was time to go.

"Yes, of course. Another time," he responded.

She hoped he wouldn't hold her to it.

"I hope you get the job!" he added.

"Thank you."

Augusta swiftly headed off in the direction of Trafalgar Square.

Chapter 17

'IT WON'T BE long before they find out. And then what will everyone think?'

The short, unpleasant letter Mary Daly had received that morning consumed her thoughts. It was no more malicious than the previous letters, but each one she received made her feel a little worse.

Just as the sender intended, no doubt.

She looked out of her office window at the rain-soaked buildings on the opposite side of Haymarket. Above them, heavy grey clouds were rolling in from the west.

Who's writing these letters? The only clue was the Euston NW1 postmark on each of the envelopes. *But what can I do with that information? Hundreds of people post letters there every day.* Mary had kept all the letters in case she needed to show them to the police. *But is there anything the police can do about them? Would they even be interested?*

She turned back to the notebook on her desk and tried to work on her report about the opening of a new exhibition at the Guildhall Art Gallery. A party had been held to celebrate the event, and it was her job to report on the attendees and, more importantly, what the ladies had been wearing.

Adorning the walls of the office were framed covers of *Aristo*'s most popular editions, which featured photographs of royalty, actresses and the latest fashions.

Mary shared the office with five colleagues, all of whom sat at desks close by and took regular breaks from their work to smoke and exchange society gossip. Between them, they held an extensive knowledge of who the most important people in London were either falling out with or falling into bed with. Mary enjoyed being privy to this information. She imagined that the behaviour of the wealthy and privileged would shock the common man if he knew about it.

From beyond a partition wall came the tapping sound of typewriters as the ladies in the typing pool helped transform the writers' handwritten articles into print.

The office felt a little calmer today. The previous day, Mary's colleagues had been keen to hear all about the airship murder. Robert Jeffreys's death had caused quite a stir, even though he hadn't been particularly well-liked.

A young police constable had visited in the afternoon and taken down a statement from her. Mary hoped that was all she would have to deal with from the police. There was nothing else she could do to help them with their inquiry.

The room hushed as *Aristo* editor Mrs Stapleton entered. She was tall and long-limbed, and looked quite sensational in a low-waisted, lilac dress of pure silk and matching cape. Her short, dark hair was lacquered into stiff curls, and a cascade of long, beaded necklaces hung from her neck.

There was a pause as everyone waited to see where her

eyes would settle. This time it was Miss Kelly's turn to be singled out.

"Do you remember me telling you about the fabulous milliner I happened upon in Paris?" she asked the young writer.

Miss Kelly nodded.

"She goes by the name of Madame Chanel. Her designs are marvellously popular there, and she's beginning to catch the eye of a few ladies over here now. Find out a little more about her, will you? Her shop's on Rue Cambon, as I recall."

"Would I need to…? Do you want me to… actually *go* to Paris?" ventured Miss Kelly.

"Yes, why not? Ask Jean to arrange it for you."

Mary felt a snap of envy. *Why am I not being asked to look up Madame Chanel in Paris?*

The editor's eyes shifted to her. *Perhaps it's my turn to be given a glamorous task after all.*

"Miss Daly," she said. "Now that the dust has settled after the airship incident, perhaps you'd like to have a little chat about the matter you raised last week."

Not a glamorous task as such, but it sounds hopeful. Could it be the promotion I asked for?

"Of course, Mrs Stapleton."

Mary pushed her feet into the damp, uncomfortable shoes that lay beneath her desk, then stood up and smoothed down her sage-green dress. She felt her editor's eyes lingering on her as she did so.

"I like the wide sleeves on that dress," commented Mrs Stapleton, "but I can't decide whether wide sleeves are here to stay or not."

"I feel sure that they are," replied Mary as she followed the editor into her office.

"Clearly. Which is no doubt why you chose to spend a month's wages on that dress."

Mary pursed her lips and felt a bitter taste in her mouth. She resented being unable to retort with a barbed comment of her own.

The furniture in Mrs Stapleton's office was modern, with smooth, sleek lines and colourful fabrics. More *Aristo* covers adorned the walls, as well as framed photographs of its editor alongside various rich and famous people.

Mrs Stapleton took a seat behind her desk and invited Mary to sit opposite her.

Mary took a deep breath and tried not to fidget.

"I've considered your request, Miss Daly," she began, "and I'd like to discuss it further. You realise, don't you, that if I were to promote you to features editor, somebody else would have to be pushed out?"

"Must they be? Is it not possible to create an extra role?"

"Where would I find the money for an extra role?"

Mary would have liked to say that this was a problem for the editor and not for her, but she knew better than to give a smart reply. "I was under the impression that our publication had been making a decent income from its advertising recently." Mrs Stapleton's plush office appeared to be evidence of that. "I hoped there might be enough money available to make it possible."

"In which case, it's just as well that you are not the editor of this magazine, Miss Daly. The finances of a publication like ours are much more complicated than that."

"My request is based purely on my own personal ambition, Mrs Stapleton. I hadn't considered how the magazine might fund and accommodate my request. However, I wished to express my wish because I have been working on this publication for five years now and feel that I deserve some recognition for my hard work and experience."

"I will acknowledge that you've been a good member of staff for this magazine, Miss Daly, but we only have a small workforce here. As such, it's rather difficult to move people about, as I'm sure you can appreciate."

"Oh, I do appreciate it, Mrs Stapleton. The day-to-day management of your staff isn't something I've considered at great length, either. After all, I'm merely a writer. However, I would like to take on a little more responsibility, and I feel I've earned it."

The editor opened a folder that was lying on her desk and began to leaf through it.

"I have a compilation of your articles here, Miss Daly, and on the whole they are very good and meet my expectations of our writers. But I must stress the phrase that they *meet my expectations*. They do just that and are in no way truly outstanding. And even though you have been writing for this magazine for five years, your work still requires just as much editing now as it did at the very beginning."

Mary bit her lip. *Has she really called me into her office just to belittle me?*

"When you asked me to attend the airship flight in your place, Mrs Stapleton, I took it to mean that you perhaps considered me to be the next most senior member of staff at this magazine."

The editor laughed. "Not at all! You were the third person I asked."

Mary tried not to flinch in response to this major blow. She took a long breath in through her nose and stared hard at Mrs Stapleton to demonstrate that she refused to be upset by the editor's callous comments. Mary was tempted to leave the office there and then but doing so would be considered impertinent and might put her job at risk, never mind the promotion.

"Perhaps I overestimated your opinion of me," she said.

This remark caused Mrs Stapleton to soften slightly, and she smiled. "Don't be too hard on yourself, Miss Daly. You're a good writer, as I've already told you, and I appreciate all the work you've done for the magazine. But at the present time there simply isn't a promotion available for you."

"Well, thank you for informing me, Mrs Stapleton. At least my position has been made clear."

"Absolutely, it has. Keep up the good work, and we can have another chat about this in six months or so. What do you think?"

If I'm still here by then, Mary thought to herself. She forced a smile, got to her feet and left the room.

Back at her desk, Mary lit a cigarette and checked the time on her watch. It wouldn't be long now until she could have a whiskey at the Chequers Tavern.

Did Mrs Stapleton really mean that I might be promoted in six months? Or did she merely say it to put an end to the conversation?

Either way, Mary was beginning to lose interest in her job at *Aristo. There are other magazines in London I could work for. I don't have to stay here.*

Jean interrupted her thoughts. "There's someone here to see you, Miss Daly," she said.

Mary wasn't expecting any visitors. "Who is it?"

"A lady named Mrs Peel. She asked if she could speak to you in private."

Chapter 18

MARY DALY STRODE into the reception area and gave Augusta a wary glance. "You look familiar," she commented as she fetched a dark green hat and coat from the coat stand. "Where have I seen you before?"

"On the airship," Augusta replied.

Mary's brow furrowed. "But you weren't one of the guests, were you?"

"I'll explain everything in just a moment," Augusta responded, reluctant to explain too much in front of the woman at the reception desk.

"Right." Mary pulled the hat on over her bobbed blonde hair, then shrugged on the coat. "I understand you want to talk privately. There's nowhere private in this building, so we'll have to go out. Is it still raining out there?"

"I'm afraid so."

Mary tutted and helped herself to one of the umbrellas in the brass stand just inside the entrance.

"Right. Let's be off."

Augusta followed Mary down the steps and out onto

the street. The reporter walked so briskly that Augusta had to break into a trot to keep up with her. There was something impatient and ill-tempered about the Irishwoman today.

"The Chequers Tavern will be opening shortly," Mary said. "We'll go in there, if you don't mind. I could do with a whiskey."

"Is everything alright?"

"As alright as it ever is."

Mary flashed Augusta a weary smile. Augusta wasn't sure what to make of her.

They crossed the busy thoroughfare of Haymarket and turned into narrow Norris Street. "Let's go through the little lanes," said Mary. "I like weaving through the yards, don't you? You see so much more of life that way. The main streets are so dull these days. I think I remember you from the airship now. You were serving coffee, weren't you?"

"That's right."

"Start explaining everything to me, then, like you said you would."

"I'm not really a waitress. I was on the airship because I was working undercover for Scotland Yard."

"Were you now?"

If Mary was surprised by this, she didn't show it. She strode on, turning left into a narrow street, then right again. They passed shabby shopfronts and the closed doorways of several night-time venues.

"What does Scotland Yard want with me?" she asked a few moments later.

"I don't think they want anything from you specifically, but they're interviewing everybody who was on the airship."

"A police officer has already taken a statement from

me. I can't see what else is needed." Mary stopped and stared at Augusta. "If you're working for the police, I'm afraid there's nothing I can help you with."

"Oh, I'm not. I'm… For want of a better description, I suppose I'm a private detective. I only got involved because I also happened to be on the airship."

"I don't know what you're hoping to gain by talking to me, Mrs Peel. I have nothing for you or for Scotland Yard. And having learned that you're a private detective and were working undercover on the airship, I feel as though I should be the one asking the questions!"

"I can't tell you a great deal more than I already have, other than I was asked to keep an eye on Mr Jeffreys."

"Why?"

Augusta deduced that Mary Daly was naturally curious, given that she was a journalist. Therefore, it made sense to build a rapport by pretending to confide in her about something.

She lowered her voice to enhance the intrigue. "He was believed to have been involved in a number of dubious practices, some of which were linked to the government."

Mary's eyes grew wide. "Dubious? Government? Now, that *is* interesting."

"Well, it *was* interesting… until someone went and murdered him. I suspect he's taken a lot of secrets to his grave."

"Indeed he has."

Augusta noted that Mary had said this with some degree of certainty.

"The Yard is still trying to ascertain the motive behind Mr Jeffreys's murder."

"And you think I'd know that?"

"No, but you might be able to help us find someone who could shed some light on the matter."

"I doubt it."

They crossed Regent Street and continued on into another narrow lane.

"How well did you know Mr Jeffreys?" Augusta asked.

"I didn't know him well at all. I'd never even met him before I boarded the airship."

"But he invited you to join him for the trip, did he not?"

"He invited my editor, Mrs Stapleton, not me. I went in her place. Although I wish I hadn't bothered doing her any favours now."

"What makes you say that?"

"Oh, nothing. A small disagreement I've just had with her."

"What did you make of the flight? Before Mr Jeffreys was murdered, of course."

"I suppose I managed to enjoy myself a little. There were a few people on board who I'd met before. And I enjoyed looking out at the view. That was very impressive indeed."

"I was waiting on the table Mr and Mrs Somerville were seated at. I noticed you talking to them."

"Yes. They were among the people I was referring to. I've met them both before. Mr Somerville is a writer for the *Daily Gazette*, so it's not unusual for our paths to cross at certain events."

"You said that you enjoyed the trip to begin with."

"Yes, I did. What is it you're trying to get from me?"

Augusta took a deep breath and decided to ask the challenging question that had been lingering at the back of her mind. "Apparently, some of the other passengers mentioned that your mood suddenly changed during the flight. Does that ring a bell?"

Mary gave a derisory laugh. "I imagine the murder had something to do with that!"

"It was suggested that your mood had changed before that."

"Had it?" she laughed again. "I don't know how anyone could have been so sure about my mood that day."

The atmosphere between the two women felt frosty as they crossed a small yard to reach the rear of the Chequers Tavern.

Augusta probed once again as they stopped at the door. "Forgive me, Miss Daly. I'm only repeating what I was told. Only, it appeared to some that you had been upset by something."

Mary fixed her with her dark-rimmed eyes. "Other than the murder, I can assure you that nothing upset me on that airship, Mrs Peel. I can only imagine that the people who suggested such a thing must be involved in the crime themselves. Surely the culprit will do anything he can to deflect attention away from himself?"

"I couldn't possibly comment on that, Miss Daly. I just wanted to know if there was anything else you could tell me about the flight. Detective Inspector Fisher at Scotland Yard will be interviewing everyone in much more detail. Some people prefer to chat freely in a more relaxed conversation like this rather than being interviewed at the Yard. If there's anything at all that you wish to mention, now would be a good time. It won't be long before Detective Inspector Fisher and his colleagues call you in, and the police can be a little more serious about these matters than someone like me."

Mary's face stiffened. "Are you pretending to make life easier for me, Mrs Peel?"

"No, I'm not pretending. It would be easier to talk to

me, wouldn't it? Nobody likes being questioned by the police."

"Don't you worry about me, Mrs Peel. I'm made of strong stuff and I've nothing to hide. A brief conversation down at Scotland Yard doesn't worry me at all; in fact, it'll give me an opportunity to clear up a few of the rumours being circulated about me. Now, do please excuse me. I need a whiskey. *Alone*."

"Thank you for talking to me."

Miss Daly sniffed and disappeared through the door.

Chapter 19

"WHAT DO YOU THINK, THEN?" Philip asked the following day. "Did it strike you that either might be hiding anything?"

"Oh, I'm quite sure that they both are," replied Augusta. "But whether their secrets relate to the murder or something else, I couldn't honestly tell."

They were seated in Philip's wood-panelled office at Scotland Yard, where the smell of tobacco lingered in the air.

"Neither conversation ended well," she continued. "Arthur Thompson invited me for a drink, while Mary Daly refused me one."

Philip chuckled. "It's going to be rather difficult to get the truth out of them. I can't say I like that Thompson fellow. He seems a little too eager to please for my liking."

"Yes, he is. It's an irritating character trait, but it obviously made him very employable for Mr Jeffreys."

"And Miss Daly was quite adamant that nothing had upset her before Mr Jeffreys was found murdered, was she?"

"She ridiculed the idea and implied that the person who had suggested it to the police might actually be the murderer himself."

"But you agreed that she seemed upset that day, didn't you?"

"I did. I noticed the change in her, although I didn't want to upset her any further by telling her that."

"I'll have to speak to her myself. I hoped you might be able to find something out before I did so."

"There was something that interested me during our conversation. When I suggested that Mr Jeffreys's secrets had died with him, she agreed quite heartily."

"Is that so?"

"There may be nothing more to it, but I wondered if she was inwardly expressing a slight sense of relief that he had died. She claimed not to have known him, but I expected her to show a little sadness about his murder all the same."

"There was no sadness at all?"

"None that I could see."

"Interesting."

They paused their conversation while one of the secretaries brought in a tea tray and set it down on Philip's desk. He thanked her, then waited for her to close the door before speaking again.

"Well, here's something interesting," he said, passing Augusta a small brown envelope.

"What is it?"

"Have a look."

Augusta peered inside the envelope and saw a crumpled slip of beige paper inside. She pulled it out, then smoothed it flat with her fingers.

"Five nine eight," she said, reading out the three large digits that appeared on the ticket.

"Indeed."

"Would you like to give me some context?"

"Ah, yes. That would be useful, wouldn't it? This cloak-room ticket was found on the floor of the cabin in which Mr Jeffreys was murdered."

"Then it belongs to the murderer?"

"It may do. Or perhaps it belonged to Mr Jeffreys."

Augusta turned the slip of paper over in her hands, but there was nothing else written on it. "It might have come from a nightclub," she said, "or a theatre. A restaurant, even."

"One of those places, yes. Not many of them about, are there?" Philip laughed.

Augusta placed the ticket back in its envelope and returned it to him.

"The murder weapon is proving to be a bit of a puzzle, too," said Philip. "The knife blade was six inches long and the handle about four inches. That's a ten-inch knife, which wouldn't have been easy to hide about one's person. It's possible that the murderer tucked it inside the front of his jacket or even shoved it up the sleeve."

"Ouch! Surely he would have cut himself, if so?"

"He may have done. And he possibly cut his shirt or jacket sleeve, too." Philip got to his feet and picked up a ruler from his desk. "It's also possible that the murderer hid it beneath his jacket like this and pushed it into the back of his trousers like so."

Augusta watched as Philip completed this manoeuvre.

"Wouldn't that be rather dangerous?" she asked.

"Well yes, of course, but then we're not talking about someone with a great deal of sense here, are we? This is someone who decided to murder Mr Jeffreys on impulse. By the time he got hold of this weapon," he said, pulling the ruler out and brandishing it menacingly, "he'd already lost all rational thought, hadn't he?"

"So the murderer hid the knife inside his jacket, up the sleeve or down the back of his trousers?"

"It's not impossible. I've tried it myself."

"How?"

"As it happens, we have a kitchen knife the exact same size as the murder weapon at home, so I spent a bit of time yesterday evening concealing it about my person."

"You could have hurt yourself!"

"I did. I cut a finger." He wiggled the middle finger of his left hand, which had a small bandage tied around it. "But it could have been far worse when you consider some of the places I was trying to hide it. I might have found more if Mrs Fisher hadn't put a stop to it!"

Augusta laughed. "I suppose she was the one who had to bandage your finger for you."

"Yes, she was." He put the ruler back on his desk and sat down again. "I suppose we have to consider the possibility that the murderer may have been a woman. In which case, the knife could have been secreted in a handbag."

"It would have to have been quite a large handbag."

"Yes, indeed. Did you happen to notice the size of the bags the ladies were carrying?"

"I can't say that I did."

"I'll have to ask them about their handbags when I interview them." He began to pour out the tea. "I took the liberty of visiting Mr Jeffreys's office earlier today. It's only a minute's walk from here. I had a conversation with the lawyer, Mr Digby, who is sorting out Mr Jeffreys's affairs. He didn't let much slip, as you'd expect from a lawyer."

"Was Arthur Thompson there?"

"Yes, but he was in another room. I saw him briefly, but

it was the lawyer I was more interested in. He was deeply saddened by his client's passing, of course. The only money left to make from Jeffreys now will be from the settling of his estate. It must be a great disappointment to these legal types when they lose a valuable client. He did mention something of interest, though."

Philip passed Augusta a cup of tea.

"What was that?"

"He's been speaking to Mr Jeffreys's accountant, and apparently a minor anomaly was recently found in Mr Jeffreys's accounts. It may be nothing, or it may be something. It's difficult to know at this stage, but I've made a note of it all the same."

"Will you speak to the accountant about it?"

"Yes, I will. Another item on the list of things to do."

Augusta took a sip of tea. "There's so much to think about. You've already made a good deal of progress."

"I think so, yes. But I haven't told you the most interesting part yet."

"What's that?"

"We've a number of men investigating the passengers on the airship, and something rather interesting has been discovered in relation to one of the news reporters, Edward Somerville."

"I remember him. He was there with his wife Jacqueline."

"We've uncovered something rather interesting from his past."

"Really? He seemed fairly dull to me."

"Isn't that always the way? The dull ones are often the ones with the most interesting pasts. It's possible that he may have committed murder before."

Augusta almost choked on her tea. "Really?"

"I'll briefly explain before we interview him."

"*We?*"

"Yes, you can be my scribe. That way you'll be able to hear what he has to say for himself." Philip checked his watch. "He should be here any minute."

Chapter 20

Augusta couldn't imagine Edward Somerville looking cheerful at the best of times, but he was scowling particularly heavily as he sat in the dingy interview room. His heavy brow was lowered over his dark eyes and there was a hint of a sneer on his lips.

Augusta had hoped she would be able to quietly get on with her role as scribe while Philip did the interviewing, but Edward Somerville seemed to object to her presence from the outset.

"This lady is not a police officer. What's she doing here?"

"She'll be taking down notes from our conversation," replied Philip.

Edward continued to glare at Augusta, so she rested her notebook on her lap and stared back.

"You were on the airship, weren't you?" he said. "I recognise you. Spying on me, were you?"

"Not on *you*, Mr Somerville," replied Philip. "Mrs Peel was actually tasked with spying on Mr Jeffreys. What do you know about his affairs?"

"I know very little about his affairs. He was a successful businessman and I was honoured to be invited onto his airship to experience the future of air travel."

Philip opened a file that lay on the table. Augusta saw that it contained a number of newspaper cuttings.

"'Politician on corruption charge'," said Philip, reading the headline aloud. "The byline on this article belongs to you."

Edward peered over at the cuttings with interest. "Yes, I wrote that," he responded. "It concerned the case of Sir Henry Burden, MP for Hampstead, who was misappropriating funds."

"Looking through the articles you've written, I see that you have regularly reported on cases of fraud and corruption among men in the establishment. It's a subject close to your heart, is it?"

"Firstly, Inspector, I report on the events the editor of my newspaper chooses to cover. And secondly, yes, I do believe that people in positions of power must be held to certain standards. And if they are found to be in breach of them, it must become public knowledge." He rested back in his chair, seemingly more comfortable with the topic of conversation than he had expected to be.

Philip nodded in agreement. "And it's not just corruption, is it?" he added. "You've also reported on high levels of unemployment, workers' rights and the number of children living in poverty. Are all of these issues close to your heart?"

"Of course! These things shouldn't be allowed to happen in an advanced society like ours. One only has to look at the wealth possessed by the most affluent families and men in power, and then contrast it with the poverty experienced by the honest, hard-working people who can't even find reliable employment at the moment, to see the stark inequality. I've always believed that it's important to report on these issues and increase awareness of them. In doing so, we can encourage a fairer society."

"A fair point, Mr Somerville."

The reporter's hands moved expressively as he continued. "I'm working to establish a new publication in which I will have more freedom to report on issues of inequality. I cannot overlook the fact that the *Daily Gazette* is owned by a wealthy man, who is part of the establishment himself. I should be grateful, I suppose, that he has agreed to publish the type of articles I like to write. However, I shall always be a bit muzzled there, so to speak. In my new publication, I'll be free to write whatever I like. I shall be reporting on many more of these issues, bringing them to the attention of the working man and the aristocrat alike. I've already secured a little funding—"

"I'd like to concentrate on the reason you're here, if I may, Mr Somerville," interrupted Philip.

The news reporter scowled and crossed his arms.

"How did you know Robert Jeffreys?"

"I've met him at a number of events over the years." The reporter's tone had become decidedly sulky.

"He was a rich man," continued Philip. "A man who perhaps personified the inequality you write so passionately about."

"He wasn't born into the landed gentry," snarled Mr Somerville. "He worked for every penny he earned, and for that I admired him. People readily make the assumption that because I support the plight of the working classes, I would naturally bear a grudge against anybody with money. But that's too simplistic; it's not as clear-cut as that. I resent people who have inherited large sums of money and have never known the meaning of a hard day's work. But I don't resent men like Mr Jeffreys, who know what it is to toil and strive, and subsequently reap the rewards.

"By befriending such men, I've been able to encourage them to donate to good causes. Rich men, and rich women, too." He gave Augusta a faint nod. "Rich men and women from lowly backgrounds understand all too readily the plight of the poor, and I have successfully encouraged them to marry up their wealth with worthy causes on a number of occasions. Dr Barnardo's homes received a large donation from Mr Jeffreys after I published a number of articles about Barnardo's work. It just goes to show what can be done when the wealthy are reminded of those in need."

"Very impressive indeed, Mr Somerville. One could argue that your role has gone far beyond that of a typical news reporter. You are, in fact, someone who aids phil-anthropy."

The reporter gave a humble chuckle. "I wouldn't go quite so far as to say that, but I do believe journalists have an obligation to educate and inform. I feel pleased with what I've done so far, but there's a great deal more to do. The establishment of my newspaper will enable me to bring real change."

"In summary, then, you were friends with Mr Jeffreys and were trying to encourage him to donate to worthy causes."

"That's right."

"Did you always see eye to eye with him?"

"We bickered about politics, if that's what you want to know. But we never disagreed about anything more funda-mental than that."

"I heard that he wasn't keen on some of your more recent articles about trade unions."

The reporter laughed dismissively. "We always bickered about things like that."

"There were never any serious disagreements between the two of you?"

"No, none."

"Were you aware of any disagreements he might have had with other people?"

"I'd be foolish to sit here and say that he got on with everybody. The man had his faults, there's no doubt about that. I couldn't tell you if he was locked in a dispute with someone at the time of his death. That wasn't the sort of thing he discussed with me. But it wouldn't surprise me if he had been. He was the sort of man who could quite easily rub people up the wrong way. I'm interested to know why Mrs Peel here was spying on him."

"There was a suggestion, as yet unproven, that Mr Jeffreys had been facilitating the sale of honours."

Edward's scowl returned. "Impossible! He would never do such a thing!"

"There was some evidence that he *was* doing so, not that I've been privy to it myself. An investigation was in progress at the time of his death. Mrs Peel was tasked with keeping a close eye on him while he was aboard the airship."

"And that's when he was murdered. So much for keeping a close eye on him." He stared at Augusta, as if to imply that she was somehow responsible. "How common is it for a Scotland Yard detective inspector to be accompanied by a civilian scribe?" he continued. "It all seems rather odd to me. I don't like the underhand nature of this whole setup."

"There's nothing underhand about it," replied Philip. "I've been completely open with you and have explained why Mrs Peel was needed on the airship. This is a complicated case, and she has a lot of experience."

"Really?" Edward regarded Augusta with renewed interest. "What sort of experience?"

Augusta wanted to reply but decided it would only assist Mr Somerville in his attempt to disrupt the interview.

"Let's return to the purpose of this conversation," responded Philip. "I'm particularly interested in the time when Mr Jeffreys was having his afternoon rest in the cabin. He was there between two o'clock and half past, when his assistant, Mr Thompson, found him dead. Did you see anybody acting suspiciously in or near the cabins at that time? Perhaps you walked through that section of the airship to visit the bathroom."

"You probably already know that I passed his cabin at that time because *she* saw me." He pointed at Augusta.

"Mrs Peel, you mean."

"Yes. And of course I visited the bathroom, as did my wife. Mrs Peel can no doubt vouch for that, too. If you're narrowing down the list of suspects based on who was seen near his cabin during his nap, you can count all three of us among them!" He laughed and pulled a cigarette packet from his pocket. "Do you mind if I smoke?"

"Not at all."

The reporter lit a cigarette and blew out a large plume of smoke.

"What happened to Stella Marshall?" asked Philip.

Edward's eyes widened and he froze for a moment.

"Stella Marshall?" He appeared to recover himself, then inhaled deeply on his cigarette before folding his arms. "I need to be reminded who she was."

"You just referred to her in the past tense. That suggests that you know exactly who she was."

"If I did so, it's only because you did first!"

"I merely asked you what happened to her."

"I don't know who she *is*."

"You surprise me, Mr Somerville. And just as I was starting to feel rather impressed by you. I happen to know that Miss Stella Marshall was a very close friend of yours."

Several small expressions flickered across Edward's face as he considered how to react. "Oh, Stella Marshall... I'm sorry," he screwed his eyes shut and rubbed at his brow. "It still upsets me so much that I've tried hard to forget her name. The memory of it is still too..."

Philip gave Augusta an exasperated look.

"You do recall her, then, Mr Somerville?"

The reporter leaned forward onto the table, pinching the bridge of his nose. "Yes, of course I recall her. She was a good friend of mine and is greatly missed."

"What happened to her?"

"What *did* happen to her? That's the question! I have no idea. She disappeared one evening while walking home. It was absolutely horrendous. We searched everywhere and then your colleagues searched everywhere. Eventually, they found her."

"In a ditch in a rural lane near Enfield," clarified Philip. "That was seven years ago, shortly before the war."

"Yes, shortly before the war."

He leaned back in his chair and regarded Philip sternly. "I can't understand why there should be any need to mention her death now. I was questioned about it by your colleagues at the time."

"You and your friends."

"Yes, and we were all found to be innocent. We weren't charged. In fact, there was never any mention of charging us."

"What do you think happened to her?"

"Some depraved miscreant got hold of her as she walked home. That's the only possibility I can think of."

"You're a married man, Mr Somerville."

Edward rubbed his brow again. "Yes, I'm a married man. What does that have to do with anything?"

"And you were married at the time of Stella Marshall's murder."

"Yes, I was. I don't want you wasting any time playing games with me, Inspector, so I'll be straight with you. I did have a brief affair with her, and I know what it looks like. It looks as though I might have wanted her out the way. But the affair had come to an end by the time of her murder. Now, I'm not going to sit here and plead with you the way I did with your colleagues back then. The decision was made that no further action needed to be taken, and that was the end of it. I don't see why I needed to be dragged in here and hauled over the coals for something that happened in the distant past."

"The case remains unsolved, Mr Somerville. Some of our men have started looking into it again. It's relevant because a man was murdered on an airship a few days ago, and I'm sure you'll agree that someone who has done this sort of thing before would make for a likely suspect."

Chapter 21

"Ma'am?" inquired Mrs Curran. "Are you alright?"

The housekeeper was a distant blur through Jacqueline Somerville's tears. "Yes, I'm fine. Just leave me be."

As Mrs Curran left the room, Jacqueline raised herself up from her cushioned chaise longue and stumbled over to the large windows that overlooked the garden. The thick rug felt soft beneath her bare feet as she pulled her silk shawl tighter around her body. Fresh tears began rolling down her face.

When will my work ever be accepted?

Even though she had ripped the letter into tiny pieces, its words were still ringing out in her head: 'We have carefully considered your work, but regretfully we have decided that it is not suitable for publishing with us at the present time.'

How many rejection letters have I received now?

Jacqueline had lost count. She had kept the first few, thinking they would serve as amusing mementos when her work was finally published. Something for the successful poet to show people to prove that the struggle had once been real. But now it felt far too real.

Her tears eventually subsided as she pulled her hair over one shoulder and stroked it, as though it were a precious pet. Outside, the sky was a leaden grey and orange leaves were floating down from the cherry tree. She watched a blackbird hopping about on the lawn and felt a heavy weight in her chest.

Should I spend my time doing something else? I don't know how to do anything else!

Poetry was all she had ever wanted to write. She would never be able to produce the type of lengthy articles her husband did. She couldn't face the idea of all that research or having to speak to lots of different people… or working to a deadline and being constantly under pressure. That wasn't her at all. She would crumple if she had to deal with any such thing. Besides, her own words flowed from her readily, naturally; as if she had been born to do nothing else.

She walked over to her writing desk and ran her fingers over the smooth, antique oak. A treasured possession, it had once belonged to her grandmother. Jacqueline had written most of her poetry here.

Poetry was subjective, and she knew she couldn't expect everyone to like her work. But she wasn't *bad* at it. She had won a poetry competition once and various people had told her that her work was good. *So why can't it be published?*

Jacqueline had submitted her poems to countless publishers, periodicals and magazines. She knew she shouldn't give up, but she simply couldn't face being turned down anymore. She felt weary. *Why do I feel so tired all the time?* There had been a time when she had enjoyed socialising. *I'm only young. So why do I feel like an old lady?*

She dabbed at her eyes with her handkerchief and tried to think happy thoughts. *How can I think happy thoughts? What could possibly be happy about this world?*

Mrs Curran probably thought she was spoiled. The housekeeper probably thought she was rich, too, but Jacqueline wasn't as wealthy as she'd have liked to be. *If only I could sell my poetry, I could make a bit of money for myself. Then I could buy whatever I liked without having to ask for Edward's approval first.*

Jacqueline walked back over to her chaise longue and plumped up the cushions. Just as she was about to lie down, the door opened and her husband appeared, wearing a thunderous expression on his face.

"Edward?"

"What's the matter?" he barked.

The sight of her with red, swollen eyes appeared to have angered him.

"Oh, it's nothing."

"It's clearly *something*. Look at you, you've been crying. Was it another rejection letter?"

She nodded and bit her lip to prevent herself from bursting into tears again.

He tutted and walked out of the room.

She followed him into his study. "Why are you home at this hour?" she asked.

He slumped into the chair behind his desk.

"I was called in to Scotland Yard. They'll call you in before long, too. They're questioning everyone about Robert Jeffreys."

She shivered at the thought of being questioned. "What sort of questions did they ask you?"

"Oh, all the predictable stuff. Trying to find out if I bore Jeffreys some sort of grudge and decided to stab him

because of it. Even if I had, I was hardly going to admit it
to them, was I?"

"But you didn't, did you?"

"Of course I didn't! But they'll ask you the same thing,
so be prepared for it."

"I don't know how to prepare for it. I'm worried that
I'll somehow appear guilty, even though I'm not."

"They always know what they're looking for. That's
what worries me the most."

"Why?"

"Because their aim is to unsettle you."

"How?"

"Just with the questions they ask. Anyway, I don't want
to talk about it any longer. The whole thing has put me in
a foul mood."

"It's not like you to be unsettled, darling."

"Isn't it? Perhaps you don't know me very well after
all."

"Of course I know you well. I'm your wife! I also know
that this is the first time you've ever come home early."

"I've a lot to think about, Jacqueline. I need some time
to myself."

She walked over to him and rested a hand on his shoulder. "Perhaps we could go for a walk on the heath and get
some fresh air together. That will make us both feel
better."

Edward shrugged his shoulder away and Jacqueline felt
her lower lip begin to wobble. She stepped back to avoid
showing how much his gesture had upset her.

"Did you not hear what I just said?" he replied. "I
don't want to go for a walk. I need some quiet time here by
myself. There's no need to be so clingy just because
another publisher has turned you down."

"I'm not clingy, I'm upset! And quite rightly so. You have no idea what it's like to be constantly turned down by publishers, magazines and your own husband."

"*I've* turned you down?" He laughed. "Just because I didn't want to take a walk with you?"

"I feel like you don't want to do anything with me anymore."

"Of course I do, but I'm busy. I have a demanding job and I'm also trying to set up my own newspaper."

"As you often remind me!"

"At least I'm occupying myself with something useful rather than moping around. If you're determined to be a poet, you'll have to get used to rejection. It happens to everybody, I'm afraid; all the most successful writers have been through it. You just have to shrug it off and accept that it takes time to find a publisher who will accept your work. And once they do, you'll have the chance to make your mark. Then hopefully all the ones who have rejected you in the past will regret it."

This thought brought Jacqueline some comfort. "I'd love them to regret it!"

"Good. Why not go and write another stanza or two now? Just make sure it's good enough for those publishers to regret turning you away!"

"I'm not in the mood to write now."

He groaned. "Why not?"

"Because I'm worried about Scotland Yard. What if they want to speak to me?"

"Just tell them the truth. That's what I did."

"Tell them everything?"

"Yes! Just answer their questions truthfully. They'll try to unsettle you, but they do that with everyone. Now, I really need some peace and quiet, Jacqueline."

"Of course." She left his study and closed the door behind her.

Just tell them the truth.

Can I really do that? Will they know if I'm lying?

Chapter 22

AUGUSTA LIKED the little shop on Great Russell Street as soon as she saw it. Its paned bow window and narrow door were painted dark green. Printed in gold lettering above the window were the words: 'H. W. Matravers: Magic Tricks'.

She peered in through one of the tiny window panes to see dusty empty shelves along the nearest wall. Further back, the shop was cloaked in darkness.

"Mrs Peel?" came a voice from behind her.

She turned to see an out-of-breath young man dressed in tweed.

"Sorry I'm late. I'm Bertie Elman, the agent. I hear you're Lady Hereford's friend."

"That's right."

"Let me show you around." He pulled a bunch of keys from his pocket, climbed the steps to the door and unlocked it. "It's a charming little place," he said, stepping back to allow her inside first. "Perfect for a bookshop, I'd say."

Although Augusta wasn't always inclined to concur

with letting agents, she had to agree with this one. She could picture shelves of second-hand books on the walls and a well-arranged display in the bow window. A wooden staircase led up to a galleried storey above the shop floor. Although it was old and empty, it somehow felt cosy and welcoming.

"That's a busy street outside," commented Mr Elman. "Lots of potential customers walking past, and practically opposite the British Museum! You couldn't wish for a better location, could you?"

"This was once a magic shop?"

"Yes. Old Matravers was here for years. He sold all sorts of magic tricks and novelties. Great little place, it was. He had to retire earlier this year due to ill health. He's moved down to the coast to live with his daughter and her husband."

Augusta walked toward the counter at the back of the shop. Beyond it was a door.

"Would you like to look out the back?" he asked.

"Yes, please. Is there much space back there?" She would need enough room for her workshop.

The agent slipped behind the counter and pushed a key into the door. He swung it open and gestured for her to walk through.

The back room had a high ceiling and a tall window, which let in plenty of light from the yard outside. Shelving covered one wall and a shabby, Formica-topped table sat in the centre of the room.

"Not the best view in the world," admitted the agent, gesturing at the tall brick walls beyond the window.

"But at least it's daylight," replied Augusta with a smile. "I would have my workshop in here, you see, and my current workshop is in the basement."

"This would be a step up for you, then."

"Absolutely. What's the rent?"

"Eight pounds a week, with rates on top."

Augusta felt her heart sink. *Where will I ever find that sort of money?*

"It's a nice place. I like it." She could hear the resigned tone in her voice; the acknowledgement that she would never be able to rent such prestigious premises.

"Perfect for a bookshop. There are quite a few in this area, which means that people often come here specifically looking for books. That's the reputation Bloomsbury has, I suppose. And there would be so much trade from people passing by. The popularity of the location is reflected in the rent, of course."

"Is there any room for negotiation?"

He grimaced. "Unlikely, I should say. Sir Pritchard is the landlord. He owns a lot of property in Bloomsbury, and I'd say that he's quite fair with the rents he charges. He knows what he can get for a place without overpricing it. Someone will snap it up soon."

"Yes," said Augusta sadly. "I'm sure someone will."

Augusta made her way home, passing the large townhouses on Montague Street as she headed toward Russell Square. The shop was just a ten-minute walk from her home. Everything about it was perfect. Despite that, she would have to look for cheaper premises, which would inevitably mean a quieter location. If fewer people were passing her door, she would attract fewer customers. She could advertise, but that would also cost money.

Is it worth taking out a loan to cover the rent? she pondered. *Only if I can make the money back quickly. Is it possible?*

Lots of considerations arose in Augusta's mind. What had begun as an enthusiastic idea seemed to have become a troublesome reality. She reminded herself that the magic shop was only the first place she had seen. Perhaps there would be others that were cheaper but just as suitable. The problem was, she had already pictured herself there. She could already imagine repairing books in the little back room and serving customers at the counter. It was difficult to imagine being anywhere else.

The trees of Russell Square were the colour of gold, red and burnt umber. The breeze whisked the fallen leaves around her feet as she cut across the square to her home.

Augusta was looking forward to a quieter day, as the previous day's encounter with Edward Somerville had left her feeling a little bruised. She hadn't liked the manner in which he had lashed out at her. She knew she shouldn't have let it bother her, but for some reason it had. For all his talk of worthy causes, she didn't consider him to be a particularly pleasant man.

Is he a murderer? It's certainly possible.

Augusta called in at the newsagents at the bottom of Marchmont Street and bought a newspaper. Then she made her way up to her flat to make a cup of coffee to take down to the workshop.

As she waited for the water to boil, she leafed through the newspaper and read a few stories aloud to Sparky. She knew he enjoyed the sound of her voice and loved the way he cocked his little head at an angle as she read out even the dullest of stories about the stock markets.

The news of Mr Jeffreys's death still occupied several column inches. It seemed the airship murder had caught the public imagination. She skimmed the article, which imparted nothing new, but when she turned the page to continue the story an intriguing photograph caught her attention.

It showed Robert Jeffreys and Edward Somerville in

what appeared to be a glamorous location, such as a fancy restaurant or nightclub. Between them stood a woman wearing a fur stole and a sparkling diamanté headband. She looked about forty years of age and was flashing a wide smile, revealing two sets of perfect teeth. Augusta read the caption beneath the photograph, but only the men were named.

Who is this woman?

Chapter 23

A TELEPHONE HAD FINALLY BEEN INSTALLED on the table beside Augusta's front door. She lifted the earpiece, dialled the operator and asked to be put through to Scotland Yard. Her call eventually reached the telephone on Philip's desk.

"Detective Inspector Fisher," he said in an official tone.

"Hello, Philip. It's Augusta."

"Augusta! The new telephone works, then?"

"Yes. Why wouldn't it?"

"Well, they don't always. Are you ringing me to test it out or do you have some news?"

"I found some new information on page six of today's *Daily News*. I suggest you take a look at it."

"Bear with me a moment. I'll ask around the office to see if anyone has a copy."

Augusta heard the receiver being placed down on his desk and listened to the murmur of background noise before there was a crackling sound and his voice returned.

"Got it. Page six, you say?"

"Yes."

"I need my spectacles." There was a scrabbling noise,

then he spoke again. "What is it I'm I looking for? I see there's an article about Robert Jeffreys. Those Fleet Street hacks are trying to solve the crime themselves by the looks of things."

"There's even a photograph of one of those Fleet Street hacks, Edward Somerville. He's pictured there with Mr Jeffreys."

"Not on this page."

"Which page are you on?"

"Six."

"You can't be."

"Oh, I thought I was. Sorry, page five. Let me get to six... Oh yes, I see it now! Jeffreys and Somerville looking very jolly indeed."

"Who's the lady in the picture?"

"I've no idea. It must say somewhere..."

"It doesn't."

"You've already checked?"

"Yes. Her name isn't in the caption and it isn't mentioned anywhere in the article. It couldn't, by any chance, be Stella Marshall, could it?"

"No, Miss Marshall was younger. And this photograph looks quite recent. I'd say that it was taken in the past few years. She's rather glamorous, isn't she? I can't say that I recognise her at all. It's not Mrs Jeffreys; I've seen pictures of her. There's no chance that it's Mrs Somerville, is there? I haven't had the pleasure of meeting her yet."

"No chance at all."

"I'll ask someone to telephone the *Daily News* to see if they can give us any more information about the woman. I'd like to ask Somerville about the photograph, but I'd prefer to do so once we know who she is. There may be an opportunity to catch him out."

"Do you think he's the murderer?"

"I don't know. But a quick look through Stella Marshall's case file reveals that he was the main suspect in that case, for the simple reason that he had been involved with her romantically. Three friends of his were also questioned, one of whom provided him with an alibi. It couldn't be determined whether the alibi was truthful or not, and the case eventually ran out of steam. There just wasn't enough evidence. It must have been very frustrating for the chaps at the Yard. The case hasn't been forgotten about, though. There may be an opportunity to pursue justice yet."

"But even if he did murder Miss Marshall, it doesn't necessarily mean that he murdered Mr Jeffreys."

"Very true. It would be good to determine the truth one way or the other, however. And the sooner the better."

Chapter 24

"WHAT DID you think of the shop?" asked Lady Hereford.

"It's just what I need," replied Augusta.

They were sitting in the rose-water-scented room at the Middlesex Hospital once again. A nurse had just brought in some tea and Lady Hereford was opening a packet of digestive biscuits another visitor had brought in the previous day.

"Excellent! Bertie will be pleased."

"I'm going to have to look at other places, though. I can't afford the rent there."

"Oh dear. Is it very pricey?"

Augusta suspected that Lady Hereford didn't need to give much thought to the price of anything.

"Only because it's in a popular location. I just need to find somewhere a little quieter."

"But if you find somewhere quieter, you'll receive fewer customers."

"Yes, that's the dilemma."

"Oh dear. That is a shame." Lady Hereford took a sip of tea. "I have a few other friends with property in the area. Hopefully I'll be able to help you find something suitable soon. In the meantime, how's your murder investigation going?"

"We have some interesting characters to investigate, but it's proving rather difficult to find strong evidence against any of them."

"But you're not having to do that, are you? Surely that's down to the police."

"I suppose it's not really up to me to worry about it. I just do whatever Inspector Fisher asks of me in the hope that I can help him find the culprit. But although I shan't be judged by the results of the investigation, I still feel the need to secure a positive outcome. If we can't find out who did it and bring them to justice, it will be very unsatisfying indeed."

"From what I've heard about Jeffreys, he was a fairly unpleasant man. Funny, isn't it, that everyone's spending so much time chasing after someone who probably did the world a favour."

"Although I see your point, Lady Hereford, that simply isn't the way the world works. The sort of person who carries out an act like this could very easily do the same thing to someone else."

"Well, that's true. It's quite something, isn't it, to find the nerve to plunge a knife into someone's back?" Lady Hereford shuddered. "I just don't know how anyone could bring themselves to do such a thing. How someone can be that angry or despairing, I really don't know. Anyway, you mustn't keep yourself too busy."

"Why not?"

"You can't spend the rest of your days alone, Augusta."

"I like spending my days alone."

"Oh, it can be endured to some degree, but I think we all like having someone to share things with, don't we?"

"It can be quite nice, I suppose, but it can also be rather annoying. Especially when people have different ways of doing things."

"Ah, but the trick is to find someone who doesn't have such different ways of doing things. The trick is to find someone with whom you can happily do things together."

"That's not something I'm looking for at the moment. I really want to open a bookshop, and I'm also keen to find out who murdered Robert Jeffreys."

"One could certainly argue that you're keeping yourself busy. Quite purposefully, I should add. But busy people are almost always trying to distract themselves from something else." There was a pause as she finished her tea. "There *was* someone once, wasn't there?"

Augusta sighed and looked down into her cup. "Yes, there was."

"Weren't you engaged?"

A familiar lump rose into her throat. "Yes, we were." Augusta couldn't remember how much she had told Lady Hereford about her past.

"Lost his life on the Western Front, eh?" added Lady Hereford quietly. "Like so many brave young men."

Augusta realised she was holding her breath. She blinked away the dampness in her eyes and busied herself with her tea.

"And the difficulty now is that there's a shortage of men," continued Lady Hereford.

"I don't mind that. There are so many women who wish to marry and have families. I'm happy to leave the men for them."

"Oh, you don't mean that. Are you really saying that if there happened to be a gentleman you were fond of, you would be happy for someone else to marry him? I don't believe it for one minute."

"It's not something I choose to dwell on very much. Besides, the only companion I really have time for in my busy life is Sparky."

A smile spread across Lady Hereford's face. Augusta hoped the mention of her canary would force a change in subject.

"Do you think you might be able to bring him in one day?" the old lady asked.

"Yes, I'm sure I could. I have a little cage that would be perfect for transporting him in."

"It would be lovely to see him again. I don't know how the nurses would feel about a canary being brought into the hospital, but that doesn't really matter, does it? We should just try it and see what they say."

"I'm sure they'd really like him."

"I'll tell you who else you could bring in."

"Who?"

"Detective Inspector Fisher."

"Really?"

"I'd love to meet an inspector from the Yard! You've no idea how bored I get sitting in this room all day, every day. I'm sure he has some interesting stories to tell."

"Possibly."

"Will you ask him?"

Augusta gave a reluctant nod. "I'll ask him."

Chapter 25

"THANK you for agreeing to meet with us, Mr Thompson," said Robert Jeffreys's lawyer, Mr Digby, gesturing to the empty seat at the table.

Heart thudding, Arthur sat down and hid his hands in his lap.

Mr Digby had tightly curled brown hair, and his face resembled that of a bulldog. Next to him sat his assistant, a pale-faced young man called Mr Wilde. Also present was the accountant, Mr Ketteridge, who had smooth, silver hair and a bushy moustache. Smoke curled up from the pipe that was firmly lodged in his mouth.

Arthur wasn't sure what to expect. The meeting had presumably been called to inform him that his employment was to be terminated. It was only a matter of time before his services were no longer required. But the solemn mood in the room suggested there was something a little more serious to discuss.

He glanced around at Mr Jeffreys's artworks on the wall and the carriage clock on the mantelpiece. Arthur recalled the many meetings he had been part of in this room with his former employer. Until now, it had felt like a second home. He felt a twinge of resentment toward the three men sitting opposite him. Who did they think they were, intruding on Mr Jeffreys's territory in this way?

"Thank you for your help over the past few days, Mr Thompson," said the lawyer. "You've been most helpful. I was particularly impressed when I saw how organised Mr Jeffreys's filing system was, no doubt in great part due to your efforts."

"It's my pleasure, Mr Digby. I've always been keen to do everything possible to help the business run smoothly. Mr Jeffreys was a stickler for organisation, and that's why I conducted my work the way I did."

"The sad demise of Mr Jeffreys means that all of us will have a little less work to do once his affairs have been properly settled," continued Mr Digby. "I'm still liaising with his family solicitor regarding his personal estate, but with regard to his business affairs, the work you have carried out has now concluded. I realise it's a sad day for you now that you finally have to say goodbye to these offices, but the tragic events of the past week have rendered it necessary, of course. Not only have you lost your employment, but you have also lost an employer who, as you said yourself on many occasions, was very kind to you."

Arthur nodded sadly. "He gave me a wonderful opportunity."

"Before you leave, Mr Thompson, I've invited Mr Ketteridge and Mr Wilde to join us, as there are just a few outstanding matters we need to settle. Over to you, Mr Ketteridge."

Arthur's palms began to feel clammy. He had hoped, amid all the chaos and confusion that had followed Mr

Jeffreys's death, that the small matter they were inevitably referring to would be forgotten about.

It is small, isn't it? It isn't exactly a sum of money Mr Jeffreys would have missed.

"Thank you, Mr Digby," said the accountant. He removed the pipe from his mouth and cleared his throat. "Shortly before Mr Jeffreys's death, I had a meeting with him to discuss the fact that some of the figures in his accounts didn't quite match up. Did he mention it to you?"

"No." This was a lie, but Arthur hoped he might just get away with it.

"I see. Well, there appears to be an anomaly in the accounts for the months of July and August. Not a huge anomaly, yet one that cannot easily be explained. I wondered if you were aware of it?"

"No, not at all."

"Mr Jeffreys wasn't aware of it until I mentioned it to him. It's rather odd, because he was usually so fastidious about such matters. Absolutely everything had to be recorded, as you well know."

Arthur nodded, resolving to say as little as possible.

"I'm asking you about it because the anomaly happened to fall into the category of office administration, for which I believe Mr Jeffreys had given you some responsibility."

"Some responsibility, yes. He allowed me a small budget."

"For someone as organised as yourself, Mr Thompson, I was surprised that certain payments had been made that weren't accounted for in the records."

Arthur adopted the most honest expression he could muster. "I'm extremely surprised myself, Mr Ketteridge. I have always made the greatest effort to record every single transaction as accurately as possible." He placed his hand on his heart for emphasis. "I'm astounded and horrified if an error I made has caused a problem with the accounts. If only I'd known about it sooner I could have done something to rectify it."

"I quite understand, Mr Thompson."

Mr Ketteridge seemed to be falling for his act and Arthur felt a little smug, though he fought hard not to show any relief or delight on his face. Instead, he adopted an expression of concern.

"Did anybody else have permission to spend from this budget?" asked the accountant.

"Not that I know of." Arthur wished there were someone else he could blame.

"Anybody who might have somehow gained access and spent the money out of spite?"

This struck Arthur as the best possible explanation. "I don't see how, but I suppose they must have done. I realise Mr Jeffreys's family is going through an incredibly difficult time at the moment, but perhaps he allowed someone in his family to access the account."

"Mr Jeffreys wasn't in the habit of involving family members in his business," said Mr Digby, much to Arthur's disappointment.

Arthur spread his hands and looked bewildered. "I really can't explain it," he said. "I shall have a good think and try to recall whether I made an error somewhere. If I have, then I'm terribly sorry about it. Is it the sort of thing that could be easily rectified?"

"We'd have to find a way of making the books balance," replied the accountant. "But it would be quite useful to establish where the missing money has got to, first of all."

His eyes remained on Arthur, who was desperately fighting the urge to squirm in his seat.

Arthur released his held breath and smiled. "Do you mind me asking how much money is missing?"

"Almost three hundred pounds. A fair amount, as I'm sure you would agree."

"That is a fair amount, yes. Goodness! Please, gentlemen, allow me to go back through my records, and perhaps I might be able to help you with this. In fact, I truly hope that I *can*, because if not I really cannot begin to explain what has happened."

"Very good." Mr Digby tucked his pen into his jacket pocket. "We look forward to speaking with you again once you've looked back through your own records, Mr Thompson."

Chapter 26

"ARE YOU READY TO ORDER, SIR?" asked the waiter.

"No, I'm not," replied Edward Somerville. "I'm still waiting for my companion to arrive."

The waiter gave an obsequious nod and walked away.

Edward checked his watch. She was fifteen minutes late.

He picked up the menu again and tried to find a French dish that he hadn't yet translated into English. It wasn't easy to read in the flickering candlelight.

The restaurant was small and intimate, tucked away in a little side street close to Piccadilly. It was the sort of place people came to if they wanted to meet in secret. Sumptuous satin curtains were draped over the windows, and the deep carpet and plush furnishings served to absorb any hushed conversation.

Edward had told Jacqueline he was having dinner with his editor. She had seemed perfectly happy with the explanation.

He rose to his feet as soon as he caught sight of Mary Daly weaving her way between the tables. She wore a scarlet velvet coat over a shimmering red satin dress, and her lips were stained red to match. Her blonde hair practically glowed in the subdued light, and Edward couldn't resist flashing her a smile.

He caught the scent of Mary's expensive perfume as she gave him a perfunctory kiss on the cheek. She sat down and rested a beaded handbag next to her place setting.

"To what do I owe the pleasure of your invitation?" she asked. "It's been a fair while since we last met like this."

"It has indeed. It's good to see you again, Mary. Thank you for agreeing to meet me." Edward found himself feeling uncharacteristically flustered as her gaze rested on him. "I'll get to the point, shall I? I was wondering whether you'd seen the photograph in this morning's *Daily News*."

"The one of you and Robert Jeffreys?" She smiled. "Yes, I saw it."

He lowered his voice. "It's only a matter of time before people start asking questions." He wanted her to feel as worried about this latest development as he did.

She gave a visible shudder. "Don't say that."

"Have the police interviewed you yet?"

"Only a constable. What about you?"

"Yes, I was hauled in two days ago and they asked all sorts of questions. I didn't appreciate it one bit."

"I suppose it's to be expected when a man's just been murdered."

"I realise that, but it's the manner in which they go about these things that annoys me. They're so superior, aren't they?"

"That's their job."

"Well, I think they could perform it in a less irritating way. I shouldn't think it'll be long before you're hauled in, just as I was."

She lit a cigarette and offered him one. He gladly took it.

"Do you think so?" she asked.

"I'm absolutely certain of it."

"But I've nothing to tell them."

He gave a laugh. "That's what everyone says."

"Has your wife seen the photograph?"

"Yes."

"How did you explain it to her?"

"I explained that it was taken at a restaurant where Mr Jeffreys happened to be dining with a lady I wasn't acquainted with. I told her the three of us had a brief conversation and, for whatever reason, some chap decided to take a photograph of us."

"That's not too far from the truth."

"No. But if the identity of the woman comes to light, we'll both be in trouble."

"Both of us?"

"Yes."

"I don't see why I should be."

"Because you have a connection to her."

Mary's lips thinned. "I don't see why anyone should look into that. Surely it has nothing to do with Jeffreys's murder."

"We have no way of knowing what they'll do." He clicked his fingers at the waiter.

"Are you ready to order, sir?"

"In just a moment. Two whiskey and sodas first, please." He turned to Mary. "I take it that's what you'd like. It always used to be your drink of choice."

"It still is."

The waiter gave a brief nod and departed.

Edward inhaled on his cigarette and pinched the

bridge of his nose. *Why did someone at the* Daily News *decide to print the photograph? Was it vindictive?*

Although he worked for the *Gazette* - the *Daily News*'s main rival - he couldn't see why anyone there should wish to stir up trouble for him.

"I remember that photograph being taken," he said, "and I recall thinking at the time that it wouldn't look good if it were published. Not standing next to *her*."

"Perhaps no one will pay it any attention."

"That seems unlikely. Jeffreys's murderer has yet to be caught, and people will be looking for any evidence they can find. They'll want to know exactly who is in that photograph with him. And once her identity is known, you'll be pulled into this, too."

Mary sighed. "You really do know how to cheer a lady up, don't you? I think you need to calm down, Edward. This probably isn't as serious as you believe it to be."

"I realise that's what you're trying to tell yourself, but I fear it'll make them do even more digging around."

"Are you referring to the police?"

"Yes, the Yard. And it's not just the Yard. There's that woman, too. Mrs Peel."

Mary raised her eyebrows. "She's spoken to you as well, has she?"

"Not directly, no. But she's been helping a chap at the Yard, Detective Inspector Fisher. She sat in on our meeting as scribe, and she was on the airship disguised as a waitress. Can you believe it? Apparently, she was carrying out some sort of surveillance on Jeffreys."

"Yes, I can easily believe that. We both knew that it would only be a matter of time before he was investigated."

"But we can't go admitting anything; we're not even supposed to know about all that."

"Mrs Peel spoke to me," said Mary. "She turned up at my office a couple of days ago. The Yard must have sent her in the hope that I'd let something slip to a dowdy woman dressed like a librarian."

"Oh, but she's clever. You'll do yourself no favours by judging other women solely on the tailoring of their outfits, Mary. Mrs Peel is the sort of lady who could easily be underestimated."

"I don't judge women solely based on what they're wearing, Edward. What do you take me for?"

"Good. I've found out where she lives, just in case."

"Just in case of what?"

"Who knows? We'll have to see what happens, but we need a plan."

"What sort of a plan?"

The waiter arrived with their drinks and offered to take their food order. There was some discussion between him and Edward about the bouillabaisse, and then he took a moment to write their order in his notepad.

"I need to ask you a favour," said Mary.

Edward felt a snap of irritation. "Do I look like the type of man who can go around doing favours for people at the moment?"

"I need a new job. I have to leave *Aristo* as soon as possible. I'm simply not appreciated there."

"Reporters are never appreciated. That's why I'm setting up my own publication."

"I could come and work for you."

"We won't be covering society gossip or fashion."

"I can write about more than that!"

"It's a paper for the working man. I don't think you have a great deal in common with the working man. Although, on second thoughts, you've associated with a fair few in your time."

This was an underhanded comment, and Edward instantly regretted saying it when he saw the look of contempt on Mary's face.

She lowered her voice. "If you want me to help you with your plan, Edward, you'd better start being a little kinder to me."

Chapter 27

WITH *JANE EYRE* repaired and ready to find a new home, Augusta turned her attention to a battered copy of *Andersen's Fairy Tales*. It had been left at her door, presumably abandoned by someone in the hope that she might give it a new lease of life. Although the burgundy cover was intact, it looked as though someone had spilled coffee over it. A number of pages had fallen out and then stuffed back in at the front of the book. She would need to check they were all there before she committed to restoring it.

She laid out all the loose pages on her worktable and began the laborious task of leafing through the book to check she had all the missing pages. As Augusta worked, she thought about the photograph in the *Daily News*.

Has Philip discovered who the mysterious lady is yet?

A knock at the door disturbed her thoughts. "Come in!"

She hadn't expected to see Arthur Thompson standing in the doorway, hat in hand. The smile on his face hadn't quite reached his downturned eyes.

How does he know where I live?

She rose from her stool. "Mr Thompson?"

He walked stiffly into the room, looking around a little awkwardly. "I saw you near the British Museum two days ago and followed you here."

She felt a chill in her stomach. "You followed me?"

"Yes, you interest me. I know you're a waitress, but..." he looked around again. "I'm not sure you really are a waitress. Something doesn't seem quite right."

He's found me out. It was silly to think he'd be so easily fooled.

Augusta didn't want him in her workshop.

What if he suddenly turns nasty?

She decided it was probably best to come clean rather than continuing to pretend to be Susan Harris.

"I was tasked with spying on your employer," she said.

"Spying on Mr Jeffreys? But why?"

He moved closer. Augusta didn't like the fact that he was standing between her and the only means of exit.

"I wasn't told the full reason," she said. "I was merely following instructions. I just did what I had been told to do."

"Who asked you to do it?"

"That's not for me to say."

He grinned. "A spy! I've never met a real spy before."

"I'm not a spy, Mr Thompson. I was just doing a job for someone."

"And yet you pretended to be a waitress again when we met each other in Whitehall the other day. Why did you do that?"

Augusta quickly tried to think of a viable response. "I was asked to watch Mr Jeffreys's office and keep an eye on who was coming and going. Then I saw you and thought you might be a little upset if you discovered that I had lied about my true identity..." *Is this explanation convincing enough?* Augusta couldn't be sure. "So I pretended to be the waitress, Susan Harris, again. I'm sorry if you felt misled. It can be a little odd doing this sort of job at times. I much prefer to spend my time repairing books."

"I can see that." He peered at some of the volumes on the shelves, then surveyed her worktable and the pages arranged on it. "What's your real name?" he asked.

"Mrs Peel. Augusta Peel."

"Nice name. Have the police interviewed you about the murder yet?"

"Yes."

"What did you tell them?"

"I just told them what I saw that afternoon."

"And as a spy, I'm sure that you saw quite a lot."

"No more than anybody else on the airship."

"I saw something," Mr Thompson said.

"What did you see?"

"I saw you go through the door into the cabin area while Mr Jeffreys was having his afternoon nap."

"I did indeed. I visited the bathroom."

"Did you see Mr Jeffreys?"

"No, but I noticed that the curtain was drawn across his cabin. That was all."

"Do you think the police would be interested to hear that I saw you there?"

"By all means tell them, Mr Thompson. They already know I was in the cabin area at that time."

He pressed his lips together and his shoulders drooped slightly. Perhaps he had hoped that his sighting of Augusta would give him some sort of hold over her.

"I've nothing to hide, Mr Thompson," she continued. "I may have pretended to have been a waitress, but I was merely carrying out a job for someone."

"What if the job you were given involved a little more than just spying on Mr Jeffreys?"

"What do you mean by that?"

"What if you were sent onto that airship as an assassin?"

Augusta was tempted to laugh, but she feared that doing so might antagonise him further. She tried her best to keep a straight face. "I'm no assassin, Mr Thompson. I realise it would be much more exciting if I were, but I've already told you what I was doing there, and I told the police the same thing."

Arthur rubbed the back of his neck and frowned. "I just want to find out who killed him."

"So do I. Who else did you see going through the door to the cabins?"

"That would be telling."

"Have you told the police?"

"That would also be telling." He picked a book up off the shelf and began to leaf through it.

This angered Augusta, who desperately wanted him to leave.

"I wish I knew why you were asked to spy on Mr Jeffreys," he said.

"So do I. Do you know of any reason why I should have been?"

"People seem to think I knew everything about his work because I was his assistant, but I didn't. What I do know is that he wasn't perfect, and he had friends who may have been up to no good. But I don't believe he would ever have committed any wrongdoing himself."

"I'm sure Scotland Yard will get to the bottom of it all before long."

"I'm sure they will." He ran his tongue over his lips and placed the book back on its shelf. "I happen to know that someone on the airship has been lying."

"Who?"

He turned to her and smiled. "What's it worth?"

She shivered. "What do you mean?"

"What's it worth to me if I tell you?"

"I don't want to play games, Mr Thompson. I merely wondered who you were referring to."

He laughed. "Mary Daly, that pretty journalist from *Aristo*. She acted as though she'd never met Mr Jeffreys before, but he made an interesting comment about her."

"What sort of comment?"

"A private comment, meant for my ears only."

"You're not going to tell me what he said?"

"It was crude," Arthur chuckled, "but he implied that he had met her before. In somewhat seedier circumstances."

"Are you saying that she knew Mr Jeffreys?"

"She knew him, alright. I think she hoped he wouldn't recognise her, but Mr Jeffreys never forgets a face."

He had finally told her something useful, if it were true. "That's very interesting," she responded. "Perhaps you should let the Yard know."

"All in good time, Mrs Peel. There seem to have been a few people on the airship who were up to no good. I'm carrying out my own investigations, you see. They already suspect me, so I need to find enough evidence to prove that someone else did it."

"I'm sure you don't need to do that. The police will get hold of the culprit in due course."

"You're obviously more trusting of them than I am. I know what they're like. They quickly grow tired of running around in circles and arrest the most obvious suspect, whether there's any proper evidence or not. And that's me, isn't it?"

"I wouldn't have thought so."

"You're just saying that to be polite. You want me to leave, don't you? I notice you haven't offered me a drink."

Augusta felt her stomach turn. "I'm busy," she said, gesturing toward the pages she had laid out on the table.

"Of course, yes. You're busy…" He pushed his hands into his pockets and licked his lips again. "I need to get something off my chest," he said. "Do you mind if I share it with you? I feel awfully bad about it now that Mr Jeffreys is gone."

Augusta didn't want him here in her workshop a moment longer, but she was interested to hear what he had to say. "Go on."

"I borrowed some money."

"From Mr Jeffreys?"

"Yes, from Mr Jeffreys. I intended to return it, only he died before I could, and now I feel dreadful about it. His accountant has noticed it, of course, and I'm going to have to explain myself. It was foolish…" He shook his head and blinked a number of times. "I didn't mean to do it. It was just a silly mistake. But it makes me look like a terrible person." He rubbed his brow.

"Did Mr Jeffreys find out about it?"

"I don't know. Perhaps his accountant mentioned it to him. Anyway, I feel a little better now I've made my confession. I'm not a religious man, so I can't very well find a priest to confess to." He gave a humourless laugh. "But there you have it. I shall pay the money back to his estate, of course. And I'll explain it all to Mr Digby, the lawyer. Then the matter can be cleared up and forgotten about. I don't know why I haven't already addressed it, in fact. I suppose I've always been a bit of a coward."

"I'm sure you're not a coward, Mr Thompson."

"Mr Jeffreys called me a coward."

"That wasn't very nice of him."

"Cowards die many times before their deaths. The valiant never taste of death but once."

"Shakespeare?"

"Yes, *Julius Caesar*. Quite fitting, really. It clearly demonstrates the discrepancy between myself and Mr Jeffreys. Anyway, I shan't detain you any longer, Mrs Peel. It's been nice to meet you in your proper guise."

As soon as Arthur Thompson had left, Augusta locked up the workshop and dashed up to her flat. As she dialled the operator on her telephone, she noticed her hands were trembling. She wondered why the young man had such an effect on her.

She asked to be put through to Scotland Yard and felt an immediate sense of relief when she heard Philip's voice at the other end of the line.

"Ah, Augusta! You can't stop telephoning me now, can you?"

"I've just had a visit from Arthur Thompson, and it made me feel very uncomfortable indeed."

"Oh dear. What did he want?"

"He knows I lied to him about being a waitress. He followed me here a few days ago after I'd been to look at new premises for my shop near the British Museum."

"I'll make sure there's a man on your street tonight."

"I don't need anybody watching me."

"It's just a precaution, Augusta. We don't want Thompson harassing you."

"Perhaps he'll leave me alone now."

"Let's hope so."

"He told me Mr Jeffreys and Miss Daly knew each other before the airship trip."

"Really?"

"They met in seedy circumstances, or at least that's how he described it."

"Interesting. I was thinking it might be time to get Mary Daly in for an interview. You can tell me more when we meet. Can you come down to the Yard first thing tomorrow?"

"Yes."

"Good. We've an interesting person to interview. In the meantime, keep your door locked. Just in case."

"Thank you, Philip. I will."

Chapter 28

A CONSTABLE WAS STROLLING along Marchmont Street as Augusta left for Scotland Yard the following morning. He gave her a nod as she passed him on her way to Russell Square tube station, and she realised he must have been the man Philip had asked to patrol the street and keep an eye out for Arthur Thompson.

Augusta travelled by tube to Leicester Square, then walked down Charing Cross Road, passed through the flocks of pigeons in Trafalgar Square and reached Scotland Yard a short while later.

Philip was busy writing in a notepad when she reached his office.

He greeted her with a smile. "I hope your night was uneventful," he said.

"Yes, it was. Though there was no need for the constable."

"I can't think which constable you're talking about." He grinned. "We've an interesting lady coming in this morning, Clarissa Mortimer. She telephoned yesterday to say that she had been burgled. It's not the sort of crime the Yard would usually investigate, but I was made aware of it by one of the officers in T Division, as the burglary has some significance to us."

"In what way?"

"It occurred shortly after the publication of that photograph we discussed in the *Daily News*."

"Are you saying the victim is the lady pictured alongside Mr Jeffreys and Mr Somerville?"

"Yes, and she'll be here in just a few minutes. Would you care to be my scribe again?"

"I'd be delighted to!"

"Good, I thought you might be. While we're waiting for her, perhaps you can tell me more about Arthur Thompson's visit yesterday."

Philip listened intently as Augusta relayed her conversation with the young man.

"Interesting," he commented once she had finished speaking. "He's an intriguing young man. And he stole some money, did he? Did he say how much?"

"No."

"Perhaps it's the reason for the anomaly in Mr Jeffreys's accountants which the lawyer mentioned to me. I'll report back to the lawyer and let him know."

"Arthur quoted more Shakespeare at me, too."

Philip groaned. "Not again."

A constable appeared at the door and announced that a Miss Clarissa Mortimer had arrived.

"Good," said Philip.

He grabbed his walking stick and a file from his desk, then the pair made their way into the interview room.

"It's going to be a busy morning. After this interview we have the pleasure of another with Mary Daly."

. . .

Augusta immediately recognised Clarissa Mortimer from the newspaper photograph. She was wearing evening wear, even though it wasn't yet mid-morning. Her jaw-length hair was the colour of red wine and a fur was draped across her shoulders. Jewels glittered at her ears, fingers and throat, and she wore a strong, exotic-smelling perfume. She certainly added some sparkle to the dingy interview room.

Philip introduced Augusta as his scribe and immediately began his inquiries. "My colleague, Sergeant Farrell at T Division, tells me that the robbery at your home was rather unusual, Miss Mortimer. Can you explain why?"

"They didn't take the obvious things."

"What would you consider to be obvious things?"

"Jewellery." She pointed to the jewels she was wearing. "They didn't take these, nor did they take any money or silver... Nothing of that sort."

"Is it possible that the robbery was linked to the publication of a photograph of you alongside a man who was recently murdered?"

"Yes, it's possible. I suspect the motive of the robbery was blackmail, and that's why I've come to the police. I wanted to pre-empt my blackmailer."

"Blackmail, you say?" Philip examined the contents of the file in front of him. "Let's establish the facts of the case. Your address is in Belgravia, is that correct?"

She nodded.

"A prestigious address," he added. "It's not unusual for the residents of your street to be wary of robbery, is it, Miss Mortimer?"

"No, it's not. We've all put security precautions in place. I live in an apartment, and there's a man on the door twenty-four hours a day."

"Poor chap."

She laughed. "Very good, Inspector. It's not the same chap all the time, of course."

"I believe the robbery occurred yesterday evening, while you were out."

"That's right. I left at about seven, and when I returned at eleven I saw that the place had been turned over."

"Do you live alone, Miss Mortimer?"

"Yes."

"Can you tell me exactly what was taken?"

"My personal papers. Photographs, diaries, that sort of thing."

"And there was no sign that anything valuable had been taken?"

"No. Everything else had been left."

"So the burglar's motive was to take the papers rather than to look for valuable items to sell. Does that sound correct?"

"Absolutely."

"Why would a burglar want to take those papers?"

"They contain personal information." She adjusted her fur.

"Personal to yourself or to other people?"

"Both, Inspector."

"Personal information that could be of use to someone?"

"Yes, indeed."

"Are you able to elaborate?"

Clarissa shifted in her chair. Augusta noticed that she was becoming increasingly fidgety.

"I have to tread carefully with the likes of you, Inspector. I wouldn't want to find myself in any trouble with you or your colleagues."

"I'm only interested in catching the person who

burgled your apartment, Miss Mortimer. I need to understand his motives in order to do so. Were the papers related
to your business?"

"Yes."

"Which is?"

"If I tell you the truth, I shall be implicating myself in
something."

"I can assure you, Miss Mortimer, that I am only interested in this information for the purpose of catching the
burglar."

"Why should Scotland Yard concern itself with
catching a burglar?"

"Because of the connection to Mr Jeffreys. His is a
high-profile murder case."

"I shouldn't think the two would be linked."

"Allow me to be the judge of that. Now, can you please
clarify the nature of your business? I already have a good
idea of what it might be, but I'd like to hear it from you."

"I introduce gentlemen to ladies."

"You run an agency?"

"Not a formal agency, no. My business is conducted
through word of mouth."

"May I ask whether the late Robert Jeffreys was a
client?"

"The word 'client' is a little formal. I prefer the word
'acquaintance'."

"May I ask whether the late Robert Jeffreys was an
acquaintance?"

"I would never ordinarily reveal who my acquaintances
are, Inspector, but as Mr Jeffreys is now deceased, I can
confirm that he was indeed an acquaintance. Though I
should like that information to remain within these four
walls, please." She gave Augusta a cold stare.

"You can be assured of our commitment to confidentiality, Miss Mortimer. Is it possible that the burglar was looking for papers that Mr Jeffreys may have been mentioned in?"

"Yes, it's possible. My main worry, Inspector, is the potential for blackmail. Either of myself or of the people mentioned in those papers. I've tried to be careful, but someone clearly knew what they were looking for and has come across it. I don't want anybody making money out of this. I just want them caught."

"Absolutely. There's still a possibility that the robbery has something to do with Mr Jeffreys's death."

"I don't see how. After all, the man's dead now, is he not? What I really don't understand is how that photograph came to be published. I'm not keen on having my photograph published in the press."

"Do you know the other chap in the picture?"

"No, I don't know him at all."

"Do you remember when the photograph was taken?"

"I was first introduced to Mr Jeffreys about two years ago, and I must have met him about a dozen times since then. It could have been any one of those occasions. I can't even tell you *where* the photograph was taken."

"You don't recall that evening at all?"

"No. I'm out most evenings, Inspector."

"The person who burgled your apartment presumably knew that you were in the habit of going out a lot."

"Yes. Someone may have been watching the building, though I didn't see anybody suspicious hanging about and neither did the security guards."

"It's interesting that there should be a security guard there, day and night, yet no one noticed anything suspicious."

"I can only imagine that the person who committed the robbery didn't look suspicious. It must have been someone who appeared to live there."

"In which case, we could be talking about a well-heeled robber. Perhaps someone who knows you."

"Yes, it's possible."

"A lady in your line of work, Miss Mortimer, would usually own a book of contacts. Was that taken?"

"Fortunately, no. I always carry it with me. It's central to my work, you see."

"May I take a look at it?"

"Oh, no. I couldn't possibly allow that!"

"The name of the person who committed the robbery could be in that book. You chose to report the robbery, Miss Mortimer. Surely it's not such a huge step to permit us a little look through the book. I could get someone to make a quick note of the names, all of which will remain completely confidential."

"I can't lend it to you, because you wouldn't be able to read it even if I did."

"Why not?"

"Everything's written in code." She gave a smug smile. "Sorry about that."

"Perhaps you could explain how the code works."

"That would take forever."

"May I take a quick look at the book all the same?"

Clarissa sighed and lifted her crocodile-skin handbag from her lap onto the table. She pulled out a small book with a worn black cover and pushed it across the desk.

"Have a look if you like, Inspector. It will all be completely meaningless to you."

Philip flicked through the pages of the little book and frowned. "Yes, it's quite meaningless."

Clarissa held out her hand for the book to be returned,

and the inspector slowly handed it back to her. Augusta could tell that he was keen to hold on to it but couldn't think of any pretext that would allow him to do so. Clarissa swiftly dropped the book into her handbag.

Philip stood to his feet. "Thank you for your time today, Miss Mortimer."

"I need those stolen papers returned to me as soon as possible."

"Of course. Myself and T Division will do our very best."

Clarissa rose to her feet and made her way toward the door. Philip followed in her footsteps, and Augusta was surprised to see that he had managed to move without his walking stick.

"Before you leave, Miss Mortimer, do you mind checking the details we have for you on file? I need to make sure that we have the right address, and that all the other information is correct."

He stood beside her and held the papers up so she could check them over.

"Yes, that all looks right to me."

"Thank you, Miss Mortimer."

He bid her farewell and she left the room.

As soon she had gone, he stumbled back over to his chair.

"Are you alright, Philip?" asked Augusta.

"Yes. I just about found enough strength in my leg to do what was needed. Here, take this."

He passed her the little black book.

Augusta stared at it, open-mouthed. "You took it?"

"We don't have long before she notices it's missing and returns to look for it. You know a bit of code, don't you?" he asked with a twinkle in his eye.

Augusta laughed and nodded.

"We'll speak to Miss Daly next. Then you can take it home and have a proper look."

Chapter 29

MARY DALY'S heart was pounding as she approached the imposing brick-and-granite buildings of New Scotland Yard. Edward Somerville had warned her that the inspector would want to talk to her, and he had been right. Every day brought with it an increasing sense of discomfort.

She had received another letter that morning; short but nasty. It was in her handbag, but she wasn't sure whether she had the nerve to show it to the police. Although she had been tempted to do so a number of times, she was worried about the questions they might ask. The letters suggested the author knew something about her that she had no wish to reveal.

As she neared the main entrance, a lady she recognised stepped out. Mary immediately lowered her eyes to the ground, intending to pass without acknowledging her. To the reporter's horror, the woman paused. Mary felt a pair of inquisitive eyes resting on her.

"I know you, don't I?" the woman asked.

Mary met Clarissa Mortimer's gaze and shook her

head. "I don't think so." She turned and raced up the steps, feeling the other woman's eyes lingering on her as she went.

Did the police identify Miss Mortimer from the photograph in the Daily News? *What has she told them?*

A short while later, Mary found herself sitting in a dull room with Detective Inspector Fisher and Augusta Peel. Edward seemed to think that Mrs Peel was clever, but Mary had seen no evidence of that yet.

Detective Inspector Fisher was quite handsome in a boring, police officer sort of way. He looked rather sensible, but there was a glint in his eye that Mary felt quite drawn to. She gave him a charming smile which would have caused most men to melt into submission. But not Detective Inspector Fisher, it seemed, as he regarded her with an impassive stare. Perhaps it was to be expected. He was a detective, and likely sceptical by nature. Mary hoped there would be an opportunity to win him over yet.

"Do you mind if I smoke?" she asked, removing her cigarette holder from her handbag.

"Not at all," replied the inspector.

She lit her cigarette and listened quietly as he explained that they were interviewing each of the airship passengers in turn.

"Did you know Mr Jeffreys well?" he asked.

She was growing tired of this question. "No. As I've already explained to Mrs Peel, I was travelling on the airship in place of my editor, Mrs Stapleton, at *Aristo* magazine."

"You're quite sure you had never met him before?"

"Quite sure."

"We've received some new information since Mrs Peel's

last conversation with you. It appears that even if *you* didn't know Mr Jeffreys, *he* knew *you*."

Mary held her breath and tried not to show any concern in her face. *Where has this new information come from?* She furrowed her brow in a bid to convey an air of confusion.

"*He* knew *me*? But how?"

"That's my question to you, Miss Daly. How do you think that might have been possible?"

"I have no idea. Mistaken identity, I should think."

"An interesting theory. He spoke about you to another passenger on the airship, apparently, and it was also observed that you looked uneasy at one point during the journey."

"I really don't know what to say to that, Inspector, other than that I didn't know Mr Jeffreys, and I certainly don't recall feeling uneasy at any time."

"I hope you're being truthful with me, Miss Daly, and I shall proceed on the basis that you are. You say that you didn't know Mr Jeffreys, and that you had never met him before you embarked?"

"That's right." She kept her eyes on his as she cocked her head a little and blew a plume of smoke up into the air above her.

"We have it on good authority, Miss Daly, that Mr Jeffreys *had* met you before. Casting your mind back, are they any events you can recall at which your paths might have crossed?"

"No."

The inspector frowned. "How can you be so sure of that? Might there have been a dinner, a drinks reception, a party when Mr Jeffreys was present and you didn't even notice him there?"

"I'd say that it would have been rather difficult for Mr Jeffreys to go unnoticed anywhere."

"Is that your answer?"

"No, just an observation." She blew out another plume of smoke, holding his gaze for as long as possible. "I can't think of any events I've attended where he would have been present."

"How puzzling. Your word contradicts that of another, which means one of you is lying." He put on his spectacles and opened the file in front of him.

Mary glanced over at it, trying to read the words on the typewritten pages, but it was too far away. Detective Inspector Fisher sat back in his chair and regarded her again. They had been in the same room for five minutes now, and she noticed that he still didn't appear to be warming to her.

"How long have you worked for *Aristo* magazine, Miss Daly?"

"Five years."

"And before that?"

"I wrote for a number of periodicals on a freelance basis."

"How interesting. I detect an Irish accent. Where-abouts in Ireland are you from?"

"County Donegal. Do you know it?"

"I've heard of it. Did you come to London to seek your fortune?"

She laughed. "Are you suggesting that I couldn't have sought a fortune in Ireland?"

"Of course not. I merely wondered why you chose to move to London."

"I wanted to work here."

"Why?"

"The people, the money, the opportunities."

"When did you decide you wanted to be a writer?"

"I've always wanted to be a writer."

"Did you study journalism?"

Mary felt her patience beginning to wear thin. "I don't see what my life story has to do with the murder of Mr Jeffreys, Inspector."

"There's a possibility that it has everything to do with Mr Jeffreys."

"You're barking up the wrong tree."

"I'll be the judge of that."

His gaze was fixed on her. She sensed that the more she bickered, the steelier he became.

Mary softened her approach and smiled. "I didn't attend journalism school. A friend who worked on a magazine kindly agreed to take me on."

"Sounds like a useful friend to have."

"It certainly was."

"How did you meet this friend?"

"At a party."

"You attend lots of parties, do you?"

"Of course. I love parties!" She leaned forward. "Do you like parties, Inspector?"

"It depends who else is there." He folded his arms. "Your past is rather a mystery, Miss Daly. I'm trying to understand exactly how you got to where you are today. A woman who writes for a society magazine most commonly comes from a background of education and the wealthy middle class. I'm generalising, of course, but do you understand why I'm a little perplexed?"

An uncomfortable sensation stirred in Mary's stomach. *Is he trying to catch me off guard?*

She smiled. "Class background doesn't really interest me, Inspector."

"Nor me. But it matters to many of the people within

your circles. I'd be interested to hear how you found your success."

"Ordinarily I would feel quite flattered that you were so interested, Inspector, but given the circumstances, I wonder if you might be trying to suggest that Mr Jeffreys had something to do with my career progression. I can tell you right now that he had nothing at all to do with it."

"How about another wealthy man like Mr Jeffreys?"

She felt a snap of anger. "What are you suggesting?"

"I'm wondering if you had a patron, Miss Daly."

"What sort of a patron?"

"Any sort. Just someone with money."

"Everything I've achieved is the direct result of my own hard work."

"And I would never suggest otherwise, Miss Daly. But a patron can certainly prove helpful during one's younger years."

"Would you be asking me the same question if I were a man?"

"Probably not. I'm quite sure Mr Jeffreys wouldn't have spoken about you the way he did if you were a man, either. I must consider every suspect based on their individual circumstances."

"Suspect?"

"Everybody on the airship is a suspect, Miss Daly."

"Even her?" She jabbed a finger at the dowdy woman with the notepad.

"If you're referring to my colleague, Mrs Peel, then yes. She could also be considered a suspect."

"Have you asked her whether she befriended any wealthy men in order to further her career?"

"No, I haven't asked her that. But it seemed a good idea to ask you, Miss Daly."

"It's a ridiculous suggestion. Offensive, even. And I don't have to answer it! Have we finished now?"

Mary desperately wanted to leave the room. She wanted to go far away, where no one could trouble her anymore. *What has this nosy inspector learned about my history? And what's he planning to do with the information?*

"Whatever it is you think you know about me, Inspector, it wouldn't mean that I was a murderer, even if it were true."

"Perhaps not."

"You're wasting your time talking to me."

"If you say so." Detective Inspector Fisher folded the file closed.

It felt like too much of a struggle to keep defending herself. *If he's found out about my past there's very little I can do to deny it.* All the reporter could do now was attempt to cover her tracks.

"Thank you for coming in to chat with us today, Miss Daly," he said in an irritatingly breezy tone. "If you think of anything else that might be relevant, please telephone me."

He pushed his card across the table to her, but she left it lying there.

"I've already told you all I know."

She stood up and left the room, keen to get away as quickly as possible. But before she decided where to go, she needed to get herself a drink.

Chapter 30

AUGUSTA SAT at her table that evening with Sparky perched on the back of the dining chair next to her. She held out a little piece of apple and he hopped onto her hand to take it from her before returning to the chair. She smiled. He didn't like to perch on her for too long, but he seemed to enjoy being close by.

She reflected on the interviews she had carried out that day with Philip. There was no doubt that Mary Daly had looked a little shaken by the end of her interview. She certainly appeared to be a woman with a past. She had been vague about her early days in London, and the comments Mr Jeffreys had made about her suggested he had met her in a role quite different to that of a society magazine article writer.

In some ways, Augusta admired Mary. She appeared to have had a humble start in life, but, through hard work and determination, had landed herself a good job. Augusta could understand why she was wary about people learning about her past. Although attitudes were changing, women who had made money from associating with wealthy men were still considered to be morally questionable. Augusta had no doubt that if Mary's employers found out about her past, they would reconsider her employment. Perhaps that was why she had appeared troubled on the airship flight. Perhaps Mr Jeffreys had not only said something to Arthur Thompson about her, but had also said something to Miss Daly herself. Perhaps he had threatened to reveal her secret. If her past become common knowledge, it would no doubt be devastating for her. *Did he speak to her on the airship and upset her?* That would certainly account for the change in her mood.

"I wonder if Mary Daly knows Clarissa Mortimer," Augusta said to Sparky.

He turned his head and watched her out of the corner of one eye.

"Miss Mortimer confirmed that Mr Jeffreys was a client of hers. And we also know that he had met Miss Daly before. Was that after he had engaged the services of Miss Mortimer?"

She picked up Miss Mortimer's black book and smiled as she recalled how Philip had fished it out of her handbag without her noticing. It was bound in worn leather, having clearly endured many years of heavy use.

Flicking through the small pages, she saw row after row of small, cramped writing. The words were indecipherable; seemingly constructed from random letters.

"I used to write messages in a code similar to this when I was in Belgium," she said to Sparky. "That was probably before you were born." She glanced over at the little canary. "I wonder how old you are. Lady Hereford has never told me." Turning back to the book, she said, "I always had to make sure the messages were as short as possible. The longer they were, the greater the risk that someone would decipher them. We always used a key, which was agreed between us beforehand. The key was a codeword that gave a clue as to how the message should be deciphered."

Augusta examined a page of text. "In Miss Mortimer's case, I don't think she's used a key. The code was intended for her eyes only." The memory of writing coded messages prompted Augusta to recall the evening bicycle rides she had taken to the little alleyway in Bruges and the window she had knocked at in a certain pattern before it slid open an inch for someone to receive the message

"There are all sorts of places to hide a message, you know," she said to the canary. "If I managed to curl my hair well enough, a tiny piece of paper could be slipped into one of the curls. The hem of my skirt also proved useful. I picked out two little stitches so I could slip a small piece of paper in there. I was apprehended a few times, and I think they may have suspected me, but they never found anything. It was quite nerve-wracking, but I suppose I enjoyed the thrill a little! You won't tell anyone my secrets, will you, Sparky? Just in case I ever need to hide messages in my hair or skirt again."

Augusta reached for her notebook and a pen, and began copying down Miss Mortimer's code. After a few minutes, she felt fairly sure that she had identified it.

"The Caesar cipher," she announced to Sparky. "Quite elementary, really. I'm surprised someone as secretive as Miss Mortimer didn't go for something more complicated. Each letter of the alphabet is shifted by three places; therefore, A becomes D, B becomes E, and so on. We'll be able to decipher Miss Mortimer's names in no time at all, wouldn't you say? I'll make some coffee. It's likely to be a long evening."

. . .

A few hours later, Augusta had written a long list of names, addresses and telephone numbers in her notepad. The telephone numbers had taken a little longer to decipher, but a pattern had become obvious to her quite early on.

Robert Jeffreys's name was listed, and it was associated with two addresses. One was his office on Whitehall and the other an address in Fitzrovia, presumably his home address.

A second familiar name was that of Edward Somerville. Listed beside his name was an address in Fleet Street, presumably the office of the *Daily Gazette*, and another in Highgate.

When asked about the photograph in the *Daily News*, Clarissa Mortimer had denied knowing who Edward Somerville was. *Has she forgotten about him? Or was she lying?*

Augusta got up from her chair and walked over to the telephone. It was getting late, so she decided to call Philip at home. Hoping he wouldn't mind, she called the operator and asked to be put through to his number on the Willesden telephone exchange.

"Fisher household." The voice that answered belonged to a woman.

Augusta had been expecting to hear Philip's voice. She paused for a moment, gathering her thoughts. *Of course the telephone could be answered by a woman!*

"Hello?" said Mrs Fisher.

"Hello," said Augusta. "This is Mrs Peel. Augusta Peel. Would it be possible to speak to Detective Inspector Fisher, please?"

"Of course." The voice was warm and friendly. "I'll just go and fetch him for you."

Augusta pictured Philip being fetched from his armchair by a charming wife with a soft voice and a bow in her hair. Their son would most likely be in bed by now.

Perhaps they were spending their evening beside the gramophone, enjoying listening to music together. Perhaps there was a particular song that reminded them of when they first met. Augusta figured Philip was probably silently cursing her for interrupting his pleasant evening.

"Augusta! Have you found something interesting in Miss Mortimer's book?"

She smiled at the sound of his voice. "Yes, I have. Something very interesting indeed."

Chapter 31

"I've no idea who she is. An acquaintance of Mr Jeffreys's, I suppose." Edward Somerville tossed the newspaper back to Detective Inspector Fisher, leaned back in his chair and folded his arms.

The two men sat facing each other in the Old Bell Tavern on Fleet Street. Edward had been interrupted by the inspector while he was hard at work in the *Daily Gazette* offices close by. He resented being questioned again, even though he had been expecting it.

"What more do you want from me?" he grunted, hoping the inspector would be put off by his tone. "It's embarrassing enough that you marched into my offices to speak to me. I've a mountain of work to get back to."

"A few more moments of your time would be greatly appreciated," replied the inspector.

Edward balled his fists. *Will this police officer ever leave me alone?*

"I think you know very well who the lady in the photograph is."

The reporter was determined to deny it for as long as he could. "What makes you so sure?"

"We found your name in her address book."

Edward felt as though all the air had been let out of him the moment he heard these words. *She'd kept an address book with his name in? How could the woman have been so foolish?*

"She did a good job of trying to protect you," continued the inspector. "She denied knowing you at all when we showed her the photograph. She admitted knowing Mr Jeffreys, probably because the man is conveniently deceased. But to her credit, she has been trying her best to protect her clients."

"I am *not* her client!"

"Then how do you explain your name being found in her address book?"

"I've no idea why it's there."

"Perhaps you were a client of hers in the past."

Edward felt a squirm of discomfort in his stomach. The inspector was certain to keep hassling him until he told the truth. Perhaps he could tell him part of the story and that would be enough.

"I used to be," he conceded, "but that was a long time ago."

"How long ago?"

"I don't know. A year or two."

"That makes sense. Miss Mortimer seemed to think this photograph had been taken a year or two ago. Where was it taken?"

"I don't know. A party somewhere, I suppose. I've done nothing wrong, Inspector. Why are you hounding me like this?"

"I'm a little suspicious of the fact that you've been so reluctant to admit the link between yourself and Miss Mortimer."

"Of course I didn't want to admit it. I'm a married man! If any of this gets out…"

"There's no need for it to get out, Mr Somerville. I'm just trying to understand the relationship between you, Mr Jeffreys and Miss Mortimer. I think I have a good understanding of it now. What about Mary Daly? Is she involved as well?"

"How should I know about Miss Daly?"

"She said she had met you a few times."

"So what if she has? None of this has anything to do with Mr Jeffreys's murder."

"I wouldn't be so sure of that."

Edward decided to stare the man down. *Surely he's just grasping at straws.* The police hadn't been able to find out who was behind Mr Jeffreys's death, so Fisher was hounding anyone who had the slightest hint of scandal in their past.

How do I get the wretched man off my back? Edward needed to create a distraction somehow. He wasn't sure how well this tactic would work, but it was worth a try.

"Your problem is that you're desperate, Inspector. That's why you've come after me today. I think you need to make sure that you've explored all avenues."

"Are you aware of an avenue we haven't yet explored?"

Can I really do this? He thought of his wife sitting at home, bemoaning her lack of literary success. *Why haven't the police questioned her yet? Why are they after me and not her?*

"You're aware that Mr Jeffreys owned a publishing company, I presume?" he asked the inspector.

"Yes. He owned a number of companies, didn't he? I recall that a publishing firm was among them. Just a small press, I believe."

"Yes, a small press, but a publisher all the same. I shouldn't really do this, but perhaps I've been protecting her for too long." He gave his brow an anguished rub and was pleased to see that the inspector was looking interested.

"My wife writes poetry," he continued, "and she's desperate to have her work published. In fact, I can't get across to you how desperate she is. She's been approaching publishers for some time now and the one she most recently contacted was Jeffreys and Son, the small press owned by Mr Jeffreys. I can't tell you how distraught she was when she discovered that her work had been turned down yet again. There's only so much rejection one person can take."

"I'm very sorry to hear it. When was this?"

"About three weeks ago. Just before Mr Jeffreys's murder. This particular rejection came after a great number of others, and I believe it was the straw that broke the camel's back. I've never seen her like that before. She was totally enraged."

"She knew that Mr Jeffreys owned the publishing company that had rejected her, did she?"

Edward leaned in, as if to draw the inspector into his confidence. "Not until she was on the airship. That was when she first heard about it. The penny dropped while he was talking about his other business interests. You should have seen her face. There was something dark there that I can't say I had ever seen before."

Detective Inspector Fisher frowned. "Are you accusing your own wife of Mr Jeffreys's murder, Mr Somerville?"

"Oh, no. No, it's not that at all." Edward tried to dispel the idea that he was betraying his wife by wiping the air with his hands. "Why would I do such a thing? All I wanted to do was inform you of the connection between the two. I've been protecting her, you see, as this particular connection has not been public knowledge. But as you appear to be turning over every tiny stone in the course of your investigation, Inspector, I thought I'd give you another to turn. Perhaps I'm just feeling a little aggrieved that I've been questioned several times now and she hasn't at all. I'm no more likely to have murdered Mr Jeffreys than she is, so perhaps you should speak to her about it."

"You're not just trying to deflect attention away from yourself in any way possible?"

Edward laughed at the ridiculousness of the suggestion. "Absolutely not. I'm just giving you all the information I'm party to."

"That's very interesting. Thank you."

Have I done enough to convince him? The reporter felt rather disappointed that the inspector hadn't written anything down in his notebook. *Is he about to mention Stella Marshall again?* Edward wasn't sure he would be able to keep his temper if he did.

"I'll get someone to look into the connection between your wife and the publisher in due course," said Detective Inspector Fisher. "In the meantime, I'm still interested in unravelling the mysterious relationship between yourself, Mr Jeffreys, Miss Daly and Miss Mortimer. Perhaps you can fully explain what has gone on between you?"

"There's no need for me to explain a thing! I think it's quite obvious to you what line of business Miss Mortimer is in. And Miss Daly may have reinvented herself as a respectable lady these days, but she has a past, as you have no doubt discovered. My involvement with the two women was purely academic."

"Academic?"

Edward didn't like the way the inspector's brow knitted together as he repeated the word.

"Yes, for research! I carried out a lot of research into London's escort services. I wanted to investigate how men like Mr Jeffreys used their power and wealth to employ the services of these women. Is it exploitation? Or do both parties mutually benefit?"

"And this research became a published article, did it?"

"Yes, of course." Edward hoped the police would waste plenty of time looking for the article before becoming distracted by a new lead in the case.

Detective Inspector Fisher opened his notebook. "Where can I find a copy of it?"

Rising anger simmered in Edward's chest. "In back copies of the *Daily Express.*"

"Can you give me a rough idea of when?"

"I'd need to look that up."

"Thank you, Mr Somerville. Do let me know. Failing that, perhaps your editor might remember."

"There's no need to bother him about this!" Edward hadn't meant to snap, but he couldn't help himself. *I've had enough of this now. I'm half tempted to punch him.*

He took a deep breath, un-balled his right fist and poked his forefinger at the senior officer. "You need to stop your prying, Fisher. All you're doing is digging up dirt on people rather than actually solving this crime. I expected more from the world-famous Scotland Yard! You won't get any more from me now. If you want anything else you'll have to arrest me. Rather tricky for you, I'd say, given that you have no grounds whatsoever to do so!"

He jumped to his feet, turned on his heel and left the pub.

Chapter 32

Jacqueline Somerville had never seen her husband so angry before.

"They've got no idea!" he raged. "Absolutely no idea! They're going around accusing innocent people of all sorts, with no intention of actually solving the crime!"

"Who is? What's happened?" She sat down on her chaise longue, clutching a cushion.

Edward hadn't stopped to explain anything when he arrived home; he had just begun shouting as soon as he saw her.

"Inspector Fisher!" he spat. "I've a good mind to get on the telephone to the Commissioner. His men shouldn't be allowed to behave like that!"

Jacqueline couldn't bear to see her husband in this mood. All she wanted to do was calm him, but whenever she spoke she only seemed to make him angrier. "Have they spoken to you again today?"

"What do *you* think? Of course they've spoken to me again today!"

"What reason did they give?"

"It was that photograph in the newspaper, remember? Ever since that photograph was published I've had nothing but trouble!"

"From whom?" Jacqueline had seen the photograph of her husband with Mr Jeffreys and a glamorous-looking woman. She had asked who the woman was, and Edward had said that she was Mr Jeffreys's friend, but he couldn't recall her name. Jacqueline hadn't been sure whether he was telling her the truth or not. She knew that he enjoyed the company of glamorous women. The way he had spoken to Miss Daly on the airship was evidence of that. Jacqueline was fairly sure that he had been faithful to her, but as she watched him pacing the floor, barely able to control his anger, she began to wonder whether there was a side to him she didn't know at all.

"I don't see why a photograph in the newspaper has anything to do with it. You didn't murder Mr Jeffreys, so why do they keep bothering you?"

"Exactly! It's because they've nothing else to go on, that's why. How many of us were there on that airship? Twenty? Thirty? Not many at all, yet they've been unable to find out who murdered Mr Jeffreys. It's ridiculous. I can't understand why they haven't spoken to you yet, either."

Jacqueline was gripped by a sudden sense of alarm. "Why would they want to speak to me?"

"Because you were on the airship! You're just as much a suspect as anybody else."

"That's a silly thing to say, Edward. I had no reason at all to kill Mr Jeffreys."

"No? The fact he owned a publishing company that turned you down didn't bother you?"

"He only *owned* the publishing company. He didn't make the decision to reject my work himself."

"But you didn't bear him a grudge?"

"What's that supposed to mean? Of course I didn't bear him a grudge!"

"You may appear very mild-mannered about it all now, Jacqueline, but I see the tears pouring down your face every time you receive one of those letters. I know there's plenty of vitriol in you. It's only because I'm so angry at this moment that you've chosen to be the calm one."

"Now you're just being unfair!" A great gulp gripped Jacqueline's throat and she felt tears spring into her eyes.

"There you go, crying again."

"What do you expect when you return home and act so hatefully towards me? Your reaction to the inspector's questioning suggests to me that you did do something wrong after all!"

He took a step towards her. "I've done nothing wrong," he proclaimed. "All I've done is work hard and stick to my principles. I may have made some mistakes along the way, but I certainly didn't murder Mr Jeffreys. I'm beginning to think you did!"

"Nonsense!"

She noticed his fists clench and felt a snap of fear. *He wouldn't harm me, would he?*

Jacqueline jumped to her feet and moved away from him, inching toward the fireplace.

"Did you kill him, Jacqueline?"

"No, of course I didn't!" She grabbed the poker from the fireplace and nervously brandished it. "Leave me alone!" she yelled.

This had the desired effect, and Edward took a step back. "Would you really use that against me?"

"Only if you tried to harm me first. Get away from me, Edward, and stop shouting. I can't bear it anymore!"

He backed away toward the door. "I will. I'll get away from you for ever, if you like. Isn't it interesting to see how you behave when you're provoked, Jacqueline?"

Chapter 33

Augusta was awoken by the ringing of her telephone. Her room was faintly illuminated by the grey dawn as she wrapped her dressing gown around her and hurried into the living area, her bare feet cold on the linoleum floor.

"Alright, I'm coming!" She called out to the trilling telephone. Something must have happened for her to be summoned at this early hour on a Sunday.

"Hello?"

"Augusta!"

"Philip?"

"There's been a bit of a tragedy, I'm afraid," he replied. "Jacqueline Somerville has been found dead."

Augusta gave a gasp as she pictured the woman on the airship with the flowing hair and fine clothes. "Edward Somerville's wife? How?"

"Another knife attack. There appears to have been a bit of a struggle, too. Fancy coming to take a look at the scene with me?"

. . .

The Somervilles lived in a tall, attractive Victorian villa on a hilly street in Highgate. The area was clearly affluent and presumably peaceful most of the time. The well-heeled residents would no doubt be shocked by the news that was to greet them this morning.

A constable was standing outside the house, ushering onlookers away. A mention of Philip's name got Augusta past the constable and she was soon tentatively stepping in through the front door.

Philip was standing in the large hallway, chatting to one of his colleagues. When he saw her, he paused his conversation and greeted her. "Best not go in there," he said, nodding at a closed door. "She was found in the front room."

"Who found her?"

"Her husband."

"Edward Somerville? So he wasn't...?"

"We don't know yet. He's at Highgate police station speaking to an inspector from Y Division. He claims he went out for the evening and found her in the front room when he returned."

"Does it look as though someone forced his way in?"

"There's no sign of a forced entry."

"So it could have been Mr Somerville. Or perhaps she let someone in."

"Yes, either of those scenarios is fairly probable."

"If it had been Mr Somerville, surely he'd have run off somewhere?"

"Possibly. People react in different ways to this type of incident. I'm sure he's doing his very best to persuade the men down at Y Division that he had nothing to do with his wife's murder, but let's hope we can uncover the truth soon enough."

"He said he went out for the evening. Where was he?"

"He went to his club in Mayfair. He told us he returned home in a foul mood yesterday afternoon and argued with his wife."

"A foul mood?"

"Probably because of the conversation I'd had with him. I was following up on that mention of him you found in Miss Mortimer's little black book."

"And that angered him?"

"Apparently so. He said that he came home and took it out on his wife. He felt bad afterwards because he'd given her such a hard time. But she had become very upset, so he went out to cool his head."

"If he was at his club, someone there will presumably be able to provide an alibi."

"We've sent some men down there this morning. We'll be able to work out whether he's telling us the truth soon enough."

"It's tempting to think that he is, wouldn't you say? Why admit to having an argument with his wife if he's guilty of her murder?"

"Sometimes people like to make half confessions. They speak the truth as much as they possibly can, then change the detail when it comes to the most crucial piece of infor- mation. They find that easier than telling a complete lie." He paused and cleared his throat. "In the meantime, we've taken the opportunity to have a good look around the place. Come to Jacqueline Somerville's room with me. There's plenty to look through there."

He led the way along the hallway and past a flight of stairs to a room at the rear of the house. It was a pleasant room overlooking a well-tended garden. There were colourful wall hangings and cushions were scattered about the floor and on the chaise longue. Books were everywhere; filling the bookcases and stacked up on occasional tables and chairs. It was a calm room, clearly designed for relaxation. A constable was sorting through papers at a writing desk in one corner.

Philip led Augusta over to take a closer look. "She probably sat at this desk to write her poetry," he said. "She appears to have enjoyed writing letters, too. There's quite a lot of letter-writing paraphernalia here. Some of the stationery is personalised with her name and address on, but some is blank. She has a lot of correspondence all tied up with string and stored in here."

He opened a few drawers to show Augusta. "The other side of the desk contained the letters she was presumably intending to post. Constable Greaves here has taken them out to examine them. No stamps yet, so I suspect she wrote them yesterday and was planning to post them today. We've taken the liberty of opening them, haven't we, Greaves?"

The young constable nodded.

"What have we got so far?"

"Three letters addressed to publishers," said the constable. "And they've got poems in them."

"Any good?" Philip asked.

The constable rubbed his nose. "I don't really know, sir."

"Don't worry, Greaves, that's not important. What else?"

"There's this one, too." He handed Philip the letter in its envelope. "It's what my mother would call a poison pen letter."

"Really?"

Augusta recognised the name on the envelope. "'Miss M Daly'," she read out. "Mary Daly?"

"At an address in Ealing," added Philip. He pulled the

letter out and unfolded it. Written on a plain sheet of paper, it contained just two sentences:

Your time has run out. If I don't receive the money by Friday, Mrs Stapleton will know everything.

"A blackmail letter?" queried Augusta.

"It looks like it."

"Mrs Stapleton," mused Augusta. "I remember the name from somewhere… that's right! She's the editor of *Aristo* magazine. I remember Miss Daly mentioning her."

"Then it seems that Mrs Somerville knew something of Miss Daly's past and was threatening to reveal it to her employer unless Miss Daly paid her a sum of money," said Philip. "Perhaps Miss Daly sought a swift end to the problem. Greaves, can you send a message to Ealing police station and ask them to apprehend the lady residing at number sixty-five Eccleston Road?" He turned to Augusta. "We need to go down and see her right away."

Chapter 34

AUGUSTA HANDED Philip the little black book during the cab ride from Highgate to Ealing.

"Has Miss Mortimer been back to enquire about it yet?" she asked.

He laughed. "She certainly has. I'll make sure I leave it with the sergeant on desk duty when I return to the Yard. She can collect it from him."

Augusta pulled her notebook out of her handbag and showed him the list of names she had copied out of the book.

"Excellent," he said. "I'll have a look through this now."

They arrived at Ecclestone Road half an hour later. The sun had fully risen, and it was a cool but pleasant day. A sergeant and two constables stood outside number sixty-five, a small house within a terraced row.

"Any sign of her?" Philip called over to them, climbing

out of the cab as soon as it came to a halt beside the police car.

"There's no answer," responded the brown-whiskered sergeant. "I'm Sergeant Gilbert, by the way. We've just arrived from Ealing police station."

"Good morning, Sergeant. Detective Inspector Fisher from Scotland Yard. Have you tried going round the back?"

"Not yet." Sergeant Gilbert stood back and surveyed the row of houses. "I presume we'll need to go down to the end and back around to get there."

"Yes, that's what you'll need to do. Haven't you sent one of your men to do that yet?"

"We haven't been here long."

"How long have you been knocking on the door?"

"Three or four minutes. We knocked on the window, too." He pointed at the large bay window next to the front door, where the curtains were pulled across.

"It looks like she doesn't want to talk to us," he added.

"It certainly looks that way, doesn't it?" responded Philip. He hammered on the door.

"Is it urgent?" queried the sergeant.

"She's a suspect in the murder of a woman discovered in Highgate last night," replied Philip. "So yes, I'd say it was fairly urgent that we speak to her."

"Murder? No one mentioned anything to us about a murder!" He pointed his finger at one of the constables. "Robinson! Get round the back, quick smart. We don't want her escaping from another exit!"

"Yes, sir."

Philip opened the letterbox and called through it. "Miss Daly! Are you in there? It's Detective Inspector Fisher from Scotland Yard. I need to speak with you."

No reply came.

Philip eyed the other constable and Augusta wondered what he was planning to do next.

"You look like a strong fellow," he commented. "Fancy giving the door a kick? I'd do it myself, but I've only got one leg that works properly."

The constable glanced at Sergeant Gilbert, as if to obtain his permission.

The sergeant nodded. "Go on then, lad. Give it a good kicking."

They all moved aside as the constable took three strides back, then jogged up to the door and aimed the heel of his foot at the lock. The door gave an impressive jolt but remained firmly locked.

"And again, Bovis," said the sergeant.

The constable did as he was told, and a splintering sound could be heard as the heel of his boot met the door once again.

"Good, good." The sergeant rubbed his hands together, enjoying the sport. "One more should do it!"

Augusta wondered whether Mary Daly was cowering somewhere inside. She would most likely be frightened if so.

Constable Bovis kicked the door a third time and the frame finally gave way. The door swung inward and banged against the interior wall.

"Excellent work, thank you," said Philip, stepping inside. "Miss Daly!" he called out. "Are you in here? It's the police!"

The house was small but neatly furnished. There were two rooms on the ground floor: a living room and a little kitchen. The living room contained two easy chairs and a gramophone. A half-empty bottle of whiskey stood on the table, next to a used glass. They glanced inside the empty rooms, then Philip headed upstairs with the sergeant.

Augusta and Constable Bovis remained in the kitchen which overlooked a small, brick-walled yard. Looking out of the window, they saw Constable Robinson walk in through the gate at the back of the yard. He glanced at them and shrugged to suggest that he had seen no sign of Mary Daly.

Floorboards creaked in the rooms above Augusta's head and, a few moments later, Philip and the sergeant returned.

"She's not here," said Philip. "She must have escaped." He glanced at the door that led to the yard. "I think we all know how."

There was a teapot on the worktop next to the stove. Augusta rested her hand on it, quickly drawing it away again. "It's hot," she commented. "She must have been here until very recently."

"And scarpered as soon as she heard the banging on the door," added Philip with a shake of his head. "Why didn't you send someone to the rear of the house before you called at the front, Sergeant?"

"We thought she would answer!" he protested.

Philip stepped over to the door and opened it. "Unlocked," he commented. "She went out this way." He called out to Constable Robinson. "Are you coming inside or do you intend to keep standing out there like a lemon?"

The constable adjusted his helmet and stepped inside.

"Hello?" came a man's voice from the hallway.

Philip spun round and made his way back toward the front door. Augusta followed behind and saw a thin, bespectacled man standing there.

"Are you looking for Miss Daly?" he asked.

"We certainly are," said Philip. "Any idea where she might be?"

"I'm afraid not. She's just came round and asked to borrow my car."

"Oh, good grief!" Philip made his way out of the house. "Has she taken it?"

"Yes."

Augusta followed them out into the street.

"Can you show me where your car was parked?" Philip said to the neighbour.

"Just outside my house down there. The one with the red door."

"How long ago was this?"

"About five minutes. If I'd known she was in trouble with the police, I obviously wouldn't have agreed to it."

"Did she say where she was going?"

"No."

The other officers had joined them outside by this point.

"Did you see where she went?" Philip asked the neighbour.

"She turned right at the end of the street."

"Onto the Uxbridge Road?"

"Yes."

"Then she's headed in the direction of Uxbridge. What type of car is it?"

"A Sunbeam Tourer. Bottle green."

"Registration plate?"

"LH 6689. I told her there wasn't much petrol in it."

"How far will it get her, do you think?"

"Ten miles at the most."

Philip turned to Sergeant Gilbert. "Tell your men to keep an eye out for this man's car. You heard the description, didn't you?"

The sergeant nodded.

"And give them a call at Uxbridge. They'll need to be

on the lookout, too. In fact, all divisions will need to be on the lookout. In the meantime, Mrs Peel and I are going to borrow your car. Let's see if we can catch up with her."

"My car? But I need it!"

"Surely you have another down at the station?"

"Yes, but it belongs to the superintendent."

"I'm sure he'll allow you to borrow it under the circumstances."

"Very well. The key's in the ignition," he responded sullenly.

Philip turned to Augusta. "Do you mind driving? I haven't the strength in my leg."

"I haven't driven for a few years," she responded, feeling a turn in her stomach.

"You haven't forgotten how, have you?"

"No."

"Come on, then. Let's go!"

Chapter 35

AUGUSTA CLIMBED into the driver's seat while Philip walked round to the front of the car and turned the crank. After a few turns, the engine spluttered noisily into life and he climbed up onto the seat beside her.

"Do you think you'll be alright driving this thing?" he shouted over the noise of the engine.

She nodded. "I've driven Tin Lizzies before, remember?"

"How could I forget?"

She released the handbrake and pushed the throttle lever down. Then she gently pressed her left foot on the clutch as she released her right foot from the brake. The car moved forward.

"Are you able to drive a little faster?" Philip called out.

"All in good time," she shouted back. "There's a junction coming up."

"You've got time to move into a higher gear."

"Do you want to drive?"

"Yes, but I can't."

"Then you'll have to put up with me doing it!" Augusta made a right turn onto the Uxbridge Road. "Should I just keep following this road?"

"Yes. Let's assume that Miss Daly took the quickest route out of London. If you follow this road far enough it'll take you to the west coast of Wales. But she won't get that far without stopping to refuel a number of times."

The traffic was moving painfully slowly.

"Sound the horn!" shouted Philip. "We need to get past!" He waved his arms at a horse and cart, urging the driver to move to one side as they drove past. "I've just remembered I've a whistle in my pocket. That might help, too." He pulled it out and blew sharply on it. "Can this thing go any faster?" he called out. He leaned in and peered at the speedometer.

"We're travelling at twenty-five miles per hour," she shouted back. "Isn't that good enough?"

"No, of course it's not good enough! A Ford Model T can do forty. Come on, faster!"

Augusta adjusted the throttle and the car picked up speed, bumping over the uneven road.

The only protection from the wind was the windscreen in front of them. Augusta's eyes watered, and she wished she had a pair of driving goggles to hand.

They passed through the suburb of Hanwell.

"How sure can we be that she came this way?" shouted Augusta.

"My bet is that she wanted to get away from London as quickly as possible. If that were her plan, this is the road she would have followed."

Countryside greeted them beyond Southall where a bridge led them over a canal. As the area became more rural, the road surface deteriorated. Augusta did her best to avoid the holes and ridges, but it made for an uncomfortable ride. She felt happier, however, that the road was emptier out here. When they drew up behind another vehicle, she sounded the horn and Philip blew on his whistle. It pulled aside to let them past.

She slowed the car as they approached the village of Hayes End.

"I see fuel pumps ahead," shouted Philip. "Let's stop and ask if she called in here."

Augusta stopped the car beside one of the pumps. A garage attendant came out to meet them, wiping his oily hands on a rag.

Philip showed the man his warrant card. "We're on the lookout for a lady driving a green Sunbeam Tourer, registration plate LH 6689. We know she was running low on fuel. Has she stopped here this morning?"

The attendant nodded. "Yeah. I filled 'er tank up for 'er."

"Excellent! When was that?"

"'Bout ten minutes ago."

Philip turned to Augusta. "We're on the right track! Unfortunately, she now has a full tank of fuel, so we'll need the same." He instructed the attendant to fill up the tank. "As quickly as possible, please!" he added.

"The pump can only do it so fast, sir."

A short while later, they were on their way again.

"Do I just keep following this road?" asked Augusta.

"Absolutely. Miss Daly has no idea we're after her, does she? We'll hopefully catch up with her before long."

Augusta noticed the road was steepening. Once they were past the village of Hillingdon Heath, the car began to struggle to climb the hill.

"Come on, come on!" said Philip, rocking backwards and forwards in his seat, as if the momentum would somehow help the vehicle on its way. "Can't she go any faster than this?"

"No, she can't. She's at full throttle. The Sunbeam may also have struggled on this hill."

"How frustrating!"

The countryside had given way to a sizeable settlement. The road grew busier and more traffic began to hinder their progress.

"Hillingdon," announced Philip.

As Augusta slowed and steered the car around a sharp bend, an inn to the left caught her eye. Three cars were parked outside it, one of which was green.

"Stop!" shouted Philip.

She pushed her foot down on the brake, prompting a car horn to sound behind her.

"It's her!" said Philip, ignoring the angry driver, who shouted at them as he passed.

Augusta steered the police car into the heavily rutted car park.

"And there she is!" he exclaimed.

Mary Daly was sitting in the driver's seat in a mustard-coloured coat. Her car engine was still running.

Philip climbed out of the car. "Miss Daly!" he called over to her.

Mary looked up and her mouth fell open in horror. Then the engine revved noisily, and she pulled out of the car park and back onto the road.

Philip cursed loudly and hobbled back over to the police car.

"We should have blocked her in," he fumed as he climbed back onto the seat beside Augusta.

"I need you to turn the crank. I switched the engine off."

He cursed again and climbed back out.

Moments later, they were back on the road, the bottle-green Sunbeam still visible ahead of them. The road twisted and turned as they entered Uxbridge, and the Sunbeam swerved dangerously around an orange delivery van.

"She's taking risks now!" shouted Philip.

The road forked up ahead of them, and Mary Daly went right, as did the delivery van. The road was sign-posted for Gerrard's Cross and Beaconsfield. Augusta carefully overtook the van and continued to follow Miss Daly. The road travelled downhill, passing over two bridges, one of which spanned a canal and the other a river.

They were soon out in the countryside again, and Augusta began to wonder how much longer Miss Daly would be able to keep up the chase.

The Sunbeam was decidedly closer by the time they had turned the next bend.

"Aha!" shouted Philip. "We're catching up with her now!"

The throttle was on full, but Augusta noticed that the car was slowing.

"Come on!" he urged. "We've nearly got her!"

Augusta was overcome with a horrible sinking feeling as the power in the car diminished.

"Why are you slowing down?"

"I'm not. The car's giving up on us!"

More curse words emanated from the inspector.

The car gave a final shudder, then came to a stuttering

halt. The engine spluttered and a hiss of steam rose up from the bonnet in front of them.

"It's overheated," said Philip forlornly.

The pair watched helplessly as the green Sunbeam sped away from them.

Chapter 36

Augusta and Philip clambered out of the broken-down car onto the roadside verge. They were surrounded by rolling fields.

"I can't even see a house nearby that we could call at," said Augusta, glancing around. "We'll have to flag someone down."

Steam continued to rise from the car bonnet.

Philip tutted. "Hopeless," he said. "It's about time the Metropolitan Police spent some decent money on its motor cars."

The sound of an engine drew their attention to the road, and an orange van soon came into view. Augusta recognised it as the one Mary Daly had swerved around.

"That vehicle doesn't look very speedy," commented Philip, "but I don't see what other choice we have."

He held out his arm and the van came to a halt behind the forlorn-looking Ford Model T.

The driver climbed out. He was a barrel-chested man wearing overalls and a flat cap. "'Avin' a bit o' trouble?" he asked.

"I'm afraid so. I'm a police detective and we were attempting to pursue a fugitive." Philip showed him his warrant card.

"'Ow excitin'!" The man grinned.

"Can you drive us?"

"I ain't got room for you both in the cab. The lady can sit up front wi' me, but you'll 'ave to get in the back, Inspector."

Augusta glanced at the back of the vehicle, which was open to the elements and contained several well-filled sacks.

"Grain," explained the van driver. "It's completely 'armless."

"I should hope so," replied Philip.

"Bertha'll keep you company."

He opened the passenger door and gave a shrill whistle. A large black-and-brown German Shepherd bounded out.

"She's friendly, is she?" asked Philip.

"Course she is. She'd only be capable o' lickin' you to death."

"Good. Well, we'd better get on with it, then."

Philip clambered into the back of the van with the sacks of grain and the dog. Augusta climbed into the cabin, feeling rather sorry for him.

"Who is it yer after?" shouted the driver as they went on their way. The van's engine was even noisier than the Ford's. "Some sorta criminal?"

"A suspected one."

"What's he done?"

"*She.*"

"A lady criminal? What's *she* been up to?"

"I'm not at liberty to say at the moment. We just need to track her down for now. She's driving a green Sunbeam."

"I know exactly who yer mean!" He grinned. "Passed me by earlier, she did."

"Does this van go any faster?" Augusta felt frustrated by the slow speed and assumed Philip was feeling the same way in the back.

"I can try, but the danger is she'll end up over'eating, like yours."

"If you were able to go a little faster, it would really help."

Augusta felt a ball of impatience growing within her. Having got so close to Mary Daly, it was frustrating to have lost her again. If only she had parked behind the glamorous reporter at the inn in Uxbridge and blocked the car's escape route.

Why didn't I think of that?

The van trundled along the road and they eventually passed through the small town of Gerrard's Cross.

"No sign of 'er yet," the driver called out. "You sure she's went this way?"

"Not completely sure, but she seemed to be sticking to the main roads, so it's an educated guess."

"Where d'you think she's 'eadin'?"

"We've no idea. Hopefully not as far as Wales!"

I'm only goin' as far as 'Igh Wycombe today, though I can go on longer if that's what you'd 'ave me do. Are you one o' them lady constables they 'ave now?"

"No, just a civilian. I'm helping out."

They seemed to be making so little progress now that Augusta wondered whether she should ask the driver to stop so she could speak to Philip about the best course of action. Mary Daly had a superior vehicle and a full tank of petrol. Although she was following the main road, she could turn off at any time and then they would lose her completely.

They were driving through woodland, and Augusta reflected on the chase they had found themselves caught up in. *Is it really possible that Mary Daly murdered Mr Jeffreys and Mrs Somerville?* The society writer had successfully built a career without anybody discovering her history. If Mr Jeffreys had threatened to reveal her past, all her hard work would have been undone. Jacqueline Somerville had threatened to do the same thing; her letter was evidence of it. It looked as though Miss Daly had chosen to silence her rather than pay the blackmail money.

"Oh, 'ello," said the van driver. "Looks like she's come a cropper!"

Augusta felt a skip of delight when she saw the green Sunbeam pulled over at the side of the road. Mary Daly was standing beside the vehicle, unmistakable in her mustard coat. She watched the van approach, not yet realising who was travelling inside it.

The van slowed to a halt and Augusta immediately opened her door. As she climbed out, she was joined by Philip, who had managed to scramble down from the back of the van at top speed.

"Stay right where you are, Miss Daly!" he called out. "You're under arrest!"

In one swift movement Mary turned and ran into the trees behind her.

"I don't believe it!" said Philip. "There's no way I can scramble through the undergrowth with this walking stick."

"I'll go," said Augusta.

"Wait!" said Philip, pulling the whistle out of his pocket. "Take this and blow it as hard as you can when you find her."

"Run off, 'as she?" asked the van driver, who had joined them at the side of the road. "I'll go after 'er.

Bertha'll 'elp, too." He whistled to his dog, then took off into the woods.

Augusta followed behind, holding Philip's whistle tightly in one hand. She soon lost sight of the man and his dog and there was no sign of Miss Daly's mustard coat anywhere. The undergrowth was thick with ferns and brambles so it was difficult to move at speed without twisting an ankle, and her skirt and coat kept catching on thorns. Augusta hoped Mary would also be finding the terrain a challenge.

Making a note of where the sun was in the sky, Augusta resolved not to lose herself in the thick woods. On she stumbled, startling the occasional bird or squirrel. Now and again she paused and listened out for sounds of movement in the undergrowth – the pull of a bramble or the snap of a twig – but only the sound of birdsong could be heard.

Augusta was surrounded by large oak and beech trees. The wood had clearly been here a long time. Golden leaves came floating down from the canopy above her and the bracken was turning brown. She stumbled about, trying to find a path, but there was none she could see; not even a deer trail. Using the direction of the sun to gauge her position, Augusta surmised she was walking in a south-easterly direction from the road.

Is there a settlement nearby? Will Miss Daly get to it before I do? At what point should I decide to turn back? I can't spend the rest of the day in the woods. Perhaps the van driver and his dog have already got hold of her.

Augusta paused and slowly turned around, examining the trees that surrounded her. A flash of movement caught her eye. It was most likely a squirrel, but she decided to follow it just in case.

Then there was another movement, higher up. Something yellow. It blended in with the autumn foliage, but it wasn't a squirrel. *A mustard-coloured coat, perhaps?*

Augusta tramped through the undergrowth until she reached a broad oak tree with thick branches. It looked perfect for someone to clamber up. She paused beneath the tree and looked up at the woman scowling down at her from a branch that was just out of reach.

"Good morning, Miss Daly. You've led us on quite the wild goose chase!" She lifted the whistle to her lips and prepared to blow.

"If you blow that thing, I'll jump."

"Why would you jump?"

"I'd break my neck and then you'd be sorry."

Augusta judged the distance between the branch and the ground, which looked to be about six feet. With all the thick foliage on the ground at this time of year, she imagined that her landing would be fairly soft.

"I mean it," said Mary, pulling herself up onto the next branch.

The longer Augusta left it, the higher the reporter would climb and the more damage she was likely to do herself.

Augusta readied herself to blow the whistle again.

"I'll do it, I swear!" repeated Mary.

She was about eight feet from the ground now. It wouldn't be a comfortable fall but Augusta wagered that she would probably survive with minimal injuries. However, in no time at all, Mary was several feet higher.

Do I really want to be responsible for allowing this woman to incur a serious injury?

She watched Mary climb higher still.

"Why are you so determined to get away?" Augusta called up to her.

"I just want to be left alone," came the reply.

"And this is how you choose to be alone?"

"What choice did I have when the police came knocking at my door?" Mary stopped to rest on a branch about fifteen feet from the ground.

"You could have answered the door and spoken to them sensibly. There was no need to take off like that."

"I didn't think anybody would come after me. It's a bit of an overreaction to a small-scale burglary."

"The burglary at Miss Mortimer's home, you mean?"

"Yes. Isn't that why you're here?"

"You know something about that, do you?"

"Speak to Edward Somerville. He was the one behind it. Once that photograph was published, he panicked about what else might come out. He'd written her letters in the past, and he wanted to make sure everything was kept under wraps."

"He burgled her flat himself?"

"He asked someone else to do it. Don't ask me who."

"How did you know about it?"

"He discussed it with me. She had records with my name on, too. I worked for her, you see, although you've probably worked that out for yourself by now. You're no fool, are you, Mrs Peel?"

"I'm sure Detective Inspector Fisher will be pleased to have the burglary explained. But he didn't call on you to discuss that, Miss Daly."

"Don't tell me it was about Jeffreys again? I didn't have anything to do with his death!"

"It wasn't that, either. It was about the murder of Mrs Somerville," replied Augusta.

There was a long pause. "Edward's wife?" asked Mary quietly. "She's dead?"

If she was pretending not to know about Jacqueline Somerville's death, she was doing a pretty good job of it.

"She was blackmailing you, wasn't she?" asked Augusta. "I read one of her letters to you."

"It was Jacqueline who wrote those letters?"

This also appeared to be news to Mary. Augusta reasoned that if she wasn't aware that Jacqueline had written the letters, it was very unlikely that she would have murdered her.

Augusta noticed there was something different about the branch Mary was resting on. There were no leaves on it. The rest of the tree was covered in autumnal foliage, but this particular branch was bare.

"Miss Daly," she began, but a loud cracking sound interrupted her.

Mary had no time to respond, other than to exhibit a look of great shock. A moment later the branch crashed to the ground, taking the reporter with it.

Chapter 37

THE BENCH outside the red-brick hospital in Gerrard's Cross offered a convenient place to sit in the afternoon sunshine. Augusta sat with her eyes closed, bathing her face in the warmth. She relaxed her brow and willed her headache to subside.

The day had begun early, and a lot had happened since then. She wondered whether they were any closer to catching Mr Jeffreys's killer.

"Are you asleep, Augusta?" came Philip's voice.

She started. "You crept up on me!"

"Sorry about that. I thought you'd have heard me coming."

He sat down next to her. A patch of green sloped down to the main road in front of them.

"I've had a long chat with the doctor in there," said Philip. "He expects Miss Daly to make a full recovery. A broken leg and a fractured collarbone. All rather unpleasant."

"She'll be spending a fair bit of time out here in Buckinghamshire, then?"

"That's right. The local constabulary already have a man stationed here, and they'll keep watch over her until she's well enough to return to London for an interview at the Yard."

"I really don't think she knew the identity of her blackmailer."

"Do you feel sure of that?"

"Yes. She seemed genuinely surprised when I told her it was Jacqueline Somerville."

"We'll carry out a good search of her home, none-theless. There may be blood-stained clothing hidden some-where, or perhaps signs that she washed or burned something. In the meantime, there's also the possibility that Mr Somerville carried out the crime."

"Is he still under arrest?"

"No. I used the doctor's telephone to speak to the Yard, and my colleague told me Somerville had been released by Y Division. They were happy with his alibi, apparently." Philip shook his head. "A foolish move, no doubt. We needed to uncover more details about what happened last night first. Perhaps he murdered his wife, then went to the club afterwards to establish an alibi." He shook his head again. "Anyway, we can't sit here all after-noon pontificating. We need to get back to London. I hear the trains from Gerrard's Cross to Paddington are quite regular."

"What will happen to the police car we abandoned?"

"Gerrard's Cross police told me they'd arrange for it to be towed to a garage where it can be fixed. I'll have to apologise to Sergeant Gilbert at Ealing. Let's hope he'll be understanding about it! On reflection, he didn't strike me as someone who would be particularly understanding about such things. Would you like to walk to the train station or shall we take a taxi?"

"I'd prefer to walk. I've had quite enough of motor cars for one day!"

Chapter 38

Augusta skim-read a letter as she ate a slice of toast and marmalade the following morning. She could scarcely believe what she was reading. Although Lady Hereford's scrawl was difficult to decipher in places, it appeared she had managed to negotiate an exceptionally good rate on the shop Augusta wanted to rent opposite the British Museum.

How did she manage such a feat? Does the owner owe her an enormous favour? Or has she agreed to pay part of the rent herself?

Augusta hoped it wasn't the latter. She knew Lady Hereford was wealthy, but she wouldn't have felt comfortable about the elderly woman forking out such a large sum of money.

"This is going to be so exciting, Sparky!" she exclaimed. "A little shop all of my own! I can take you there with me each day. I'm sure my visitors would love to say hello to you, and perhaps it'll be more interesting for you than sitting up here by yourself."

The little canary cocked his head at the sound of her voice, then broke out into melodic song. Augusta grinned at him, sure that the bird had somehow picked up on her excitement.

She turned to the previous day's newspaper, which she had read on the evening train from Gerrard's Cross to London. She finished her cup of tea, then picked up a pen to complete the crossword.

Her mind turned to more sombre matters as she wondered how Mary Daly was faring after her first night in hospital.

There was still a chance that the society writer had murdered Jacqueline Somerville. Although she had seemed surprised to learn who her blackmailer was, it was possible that she was simply an adept liar. *Could she also have taken a knife from the airship galley and hidden it in her handbag?*

Her thoughts turned to Edward Somerville. Philip wasn't ready to rule him out, but the police in Highgate seemed to believe his alibi.

Augusta knew it wouldn't be long before Philip contacted her again about the case. In the meantime, she was looking forward to spending a few hours tidying up the workshop and packing her things into boxes. A move to new premises was just what she needed.

After completing the crossword, Augusta went down to her workshop to begin the tidying and packing. As she tried the door handle, she realised that the door was unlocked. She opened it, then stood on the threshold for a moment, wary about stepping inside.

Did I forget to lock up? She felt sure that she had done so the last time she was here. *When was I here last?*

So much had happened over the past few days that it was difficult to remember. Besides, it wouldn't be the first time she had forgotten to lock it. There was probably nothing to worry about.

She flicked on the light switch and everything appeared to be just as she had left it. *If someone picked the lock and gained entry, surely they would have taken something.* There wasn't anything especially valuable in the workshop, but an opportunistic thief might have been interested in her father's tools.

Augusta reassured herself that everything was as it should be and walked over to her worktable, where *Andersen's Fairy Tales* sat, ready to be stitched together. Fortunately, there were no pages missing and the book would be easy to restore.

This morning, however, she was more interested in sorting through the items that needed packing. There would be plenty of things she no longer needed.

Augusta sighed as she surveyed the clutter lying on the shelves and worktops. She hadn't realised how much she had accumulated over the years.

He could see from his position in the darkest corner of the basement that she was moving around a lot. There was something restless about her today. Drawers were being opened and various items were being stacked on tables. *What's she doing?*

Augusta coughed as she disturbed some dust, and he instantly felt a tickle at the back of his own throat. This turned into an itch that made his eyes water, but he couldn't cough and give himself away. Not now.

It was a pity he had to do this, but the situation was getting out of hand. In an attempt to solve one problem he had triggered a whole new irritating chain of events.

When will it come an end? Will they ever stop hounding me?
If only she would stop moving about so much.

His hand gripped the handle of the knife a little more tightly.

Augusta pulled numerous pieces of leather, paper and fabric out of the drawers and carefully arranged them on one of the worktops. These scraps were useful for repairing book covers, and she would need to keep them all. There was nothing to pack them into just yet, but she would ask around at the shops later for old tea chests to transport her possessions in. Tube trains rumbled beneath her feet, and she pondered the case as she settled into the sorting process.

She felt sorry for poor Jacqueline Somerville, despite the fact that the seemingly mild-tempered woman had revealed herself to be rather unpleasant at heart. Mrs Somerville might have written the nasty letters, but she hadn't deserved to die. Augusta wondered how much money she had expected to receive from Miss Daly.

Augusta bent down to open another drawer and pulled out a stack of coarse, textured papers. She recalled thinking they would be useful as replacement pages but had later decided were too rough. *Is there any use for them or can they just be thrown away?* Their beige colour reminded her of something.

The cloakroom ticket found on the floor of Mr Jeffreys's cabin.

Augusta hadn't given it any thought for some time but perhaps it was an important clue. It was possible that it had belonged to Mr Jeffreys, but it might also have belonged to his murderer.

The murderer had wiped the handle of the knife clean

216

with something, most likely a handkerchief. Men usually kept one in a jacket pocket, while women tended to keep one in a handbag.

After the knife had been plunged into Mr Jeffreys's back, she surmised that the murderer must have quickly pulled out a handkerchief to wipe his or her fingerprints off the handle. This swift movement might have pulled something else out without the murderer noticing. A crumpled cloakroom ticket lingering in a pocket or bag, for example.

The murderer would most likely have left the cabin as soon as the knife was clean, and perhaps hadn't noticed the small ticket fluttering to the floor. *An interesting theory, but can it be proven?*

The cloakroom ticket could have come from a restaurant, theatre or nightclub… or perhaps somewhere she hadn't thought of yet.

Something she had seen in the newspaper just before she completed the crossword came to mind. Augusta paused to give it some thought. *Perhaps there's something I can try.*

She felt an unexpected shiver down her spine. The light didn't quite reach the edges of the basement and it was dingy down here.

Why do I feel so uneasy all of a sudden?

This is my moment. Her back is turned! I just need to step out before she turns back round again. It's no good if she's facing me. He had discovered that with Jacqueline. *Poor Jacqueline.* His stomach turned at the thought of her.

Augusta was still facing away from him.

I have to move now.

He stepped forward, but his foot scuffed against the concrete floor.

She turned and he paused, holding his breath. Had she heard him move? He guessed not, as she soon turned away again. *Now's my chance!* He moved his other foot forward, but she was already walking away.

I need to be quick.

But Augusta was quicker. She was heading for the door, and before he had a chance to catch up with her, she was gone.

Chapter 39

AUGUSTA WAS INFORMED that Philip was busy when she arrived at Scotland Yard at lunchtime, so she had to wait in a sombre waiting room for a short while.

Philip looked flustered when he appeared.

"We can't find Somerville," he said as they walked toward his office. "I can't believe Y Division let him go. His alibi should have been scrutinised more closely, and now he's got away!"

"I hope there won't be another car chase."

"No chance of that at the moment. We don't know how he got away or where he's headed. He's not at his club or his office. And he hasn't been back to the house in Highgate, either. There's still a constable posted there."

They arrived at his office and sat down.

"I've asked them to keep an eye out for him up at Gerrard's Cross," Philip continued. "There's a chance he might visit Miss Daly, I suppose. The two of them appear to have established a friendship of sorts. Or are they lovers, do you think? I'm not quite sure, but we'll need to find that out." He paused to take a breath. "Why have you brought your umbrella? Isn't it sunny outside?"

"It's not mine. I've just picked it up from the Savoy Theatre, of all places."

His brow furrowed. "Why?"

"The cloakroom ticket."

He thought for a moment. "The one that was found in Mr Jeffreys's cabin? But that's still in this drawer." He opened it and retrieved the envelope.

"I remembered the number: five nine eight. I told them I'd mislaid it."

"And they gave you the umbrella in exchange?"

"Yes, and it obviously belongs to the person who was in possession of the ticket. Whoever it was forgot to collect it from the cloakroom."

"In which case, that umbrella may belong to the murderer."

"Yes."

"Or Mr Jeffreys."

"I suppose that's a possibility, but I'd like to think that it belongs to the murderer."

Philip rubbed his chin. "How did you know to try the Savoy Theatre?"

"I was looking through yesterday's newspaper at breakfast this morning and saw an advert for a play."

"I still don't see the significance."

"It wouldn't normally have caught my attention, but the name of the play jumped out at me."

"Which play?"

"*Julius Caesar.*"

"By William Shakespeare."

"That's right."

Philip's eyes narrowed. "Why does that seem familiar somehow?"

"Because someone recently quoted Shakespeare at me. Twice."

Philip's mouth dropped open. "Arthur Thompson?"

"While we were on the airship he quoted a line from Cassius about his master being as large as the colossus. Then the other day he mentioned a quote about cowards dying many times but the valiant only dying once."

"I'm struggling to understand the meaning behind that one."

"There's no need to. At the time it struck me as odd that he should suddenly start coming out with Shakespeare quotes. He told me they were from the play *Julius Caesar*, so I reasoned he had perhaps seen the play recently and the lines had remained in his head."

"So he could quote them to people and make himself sound clever."

"Exactly."

"But there's still a chance he went to the play with Mr Jeffreys, and that it is, in fact, Mr Jeffreys's umbrella you're holding in your hand."

"Yes, it is possible, but I recall meeting Mr Thompson on a rainy day in Whitehall shortly after the murder. He didn't have an umbrella with him, and when I held mine out for him to stand beneath he told me he had lost his."

"Brilliant!" Philip rocked back in his chair. "So it *was* him!"

"It could have been. There's still a possibility that the ticket fell out of Arthur Thompson's pocket when he returned to the cabin to awaken his employer. However, I think the ticket fell out of his pocket with the handkerchief he used to wipe his fingerprints off the knife handle. Shall we ask him?"

"Yes! Excellent work!" Philip rose to his feet and held out his hand.

Augusta laughed and shook it. "If I'm right, that is."

"I feel quite sure that you are. Don't you?"

"Yes."

"Good." He picked up his walking stick. "Let's go and see if he's still hanging around in Mr Jeffreys's offices, shall we?"

Chapter 40

"THOMPSON'S MOTIVE for murdering his employer could have been something to do with the stolen money," said Philip as they stepped out into Great Scotland Yard. "We need to ascertain whether Mr Jeffreys knew about it. Perhaps he'd even confronted Thompson about it."

"We can ask him right now," replied Augusta, stopping in her tracks as she saw a familiar figure on the approach.

Arthur Thompson had always made her feel uneasy, and now she understood why.

He greeted them with a broad smile. "Just the two I came here to speak with."

"Likewise," responded Philip. "Arthur Thompson, I'm placing you under arrest for the murder of Mr Robert Jeffreys. And I strongly suspect that you murdered Jacqueline Somerville, too."

Arthur Thompson laughed. "You can't arrest me, Inspector. My father would be bitterly disappointed. Why would I want to murder my employer? It wouldn't have made any sense for me to bite the hand that fed me."

"No, it wouldn't. But perhaps he found out about the

money you had stolen and you couldn't face the shame of losing your employment over it. Your father would have been extremely disappointed if you had, wouldn't he? So you responded by murdering Mr Jeffreys and then pretending to be the person who had discovered him. You thought no one would ever suspect you, didn't you?"

Philip took a step closer, but Arthur Thompson leapt back.

"I'd like to see you try to arrest me!"

"My advice would be not to resist."

Mr Thompson turned to Augusta. "What have you done with my umbrella, Mrs Peel?"

"How did you know that I had it?" she replied. "Have you been following me again?"

He licked his lips. "Yes."

"The umbrella is locked in our exhibit room," said Philip. "It'll be a useful piece of evidence at your trial."

"You think there'll be a trial, do you? Oh, you've got nothing on me, Inspector!"

"Why did you murder Jacqueline Somerville, Mr Thompson?"

"I didn't murder her. She *did* send me nasty letters, though."

"Saying what?"

"Horrible lies."

"What sort of lies?"

"She said she was going to tell the police that I was the murderer. She claimed she'd seen me take the knife from the kitchen on the airship. All lies, of course. She said I would have to pay her some money to keep her quiet. It was all rather silly, really. I had no money to pay her with."

"If you were innocent, you could have just reported her to the police," said Philip.

He scowled. "And you would have believed me, would you?"

"What happened to the money you stole?"

"I didn't *steal* it, I *borrowed* it. And I don't mind admitting it. I was going to pay him back. I just needed a bit extra to keep a roof over my head. Mr Jeffreys was worth a fortune, yet he paid me a pittance. Besides, he didn't miss the money."

"That doesn't make it acceptable to steal from him."

"I was going to pay it back, as I've just told you. I needed it. My parents were very impressed when they visited my flat."

"But you would have lost the impressive flat once Mr Jeffreys had discovered the theft," said Augusta.

"Not if I'd paid him back."

"You couldn't have paid him back," snarled Philip. "You didn't have any money."

"How did you know it was Mrs Somerville who sent you those letters?" asked Augusta.

"I found one of her tawdry poems. She wrote one on the airship and gave it to Mr Jeffreys. I found it among his papers when I was going through them. I'd just received the first letter from her, so the handwriting style leapt out at me immediately. Then I followed her. I like following people when they have no idea I'm there." He smirked, then continued. "I followed her from her home in Highgate one day and she took the tube to Euston. I watched her post her letters near Euston station. All the letters I received from her had a Euston postmark."

"Mrs Somerville saw you take the knife," said Philip. "If only she'd told us what she saw instead of viewing it as an opportunity to make some money, she would still be alive today." He pulled a pair of handcuffs out of his pocket. "You need to come with me, Mr Thompson."

The young man's face crumpled. "No! I won't let you arrest me!"

Philip stepped toward him, but Augusta realised it wouldn't be easy to get the handcuffs on without abandoning his walking stick.

It was then that Arthur Thompson reached inside his jacket and pulled out a knife.

Augusta gasped.

He seemed to enjoy her shocked reaction. "You're lucky I spared you this morning, Mrs Peel."

"*Spared* me?" She felt her stomach turn.

"Yes." He licked his lips again. "I was there in your basement this morning. I watched you pulling things out of drawers and rearranging them."

Her mouth felt dry. She finally understood why she had felt so nervous, and why the door had been unlocked.

"I almost did it," he continued, "but then you moved. So I decided to follow you instead."

"That's quite enough, Mr Thompson," snapped Philip.

"Aren't you happy that I spared her?"

"Drop the knife this instant! You've already been placed under arrest, and you're only making matters worse for yourself by resisting. Comply now and we can put an end to all this."

"I'd rather end it my own way," Mr Thompson retorted. Then he turned and ran in the direction of Whitehall.

"Oh, good grief!" lamented Philip. "I'll summon help."

"I'll go after him," replied Augusta, handing Philip her bag.

"You can't, Augusta. He's got a knife!"

"I'll just keep track of him for now," she called back over her shoulder as she took off.

Sprinting down Whitehall was easier than running

through thick woodland undergrowth, but there were countless pedestrians to dodge, and they did not seem happy about having to move out of the way.

Augusta was impressed by Mr Thompson's speed as he headed in the direction of Westminster. There was no doubt that he could outrun her but she hoped she would be able to hail some help along the way.

As she passed the large government buildings, Augusta caught the attention of a constable sitting in a police box. "Stop that man!" she shouted. "He's wanted for murder!"

The constable ran off ahead of Augusta and gave chase.

A few moments later, she heard the pounding of boots behind her as the officers Philip had summoned at Scotland Yard followed suit. They ran past and Augusta did her best to keep up, even though her lungs felt fit to burst. She wasn't sure how much longer she would be able to keep going.

The Houses of Parliament drew nearer and she saw the police officers ahead of her turn left toward Westminster Bridge. *Is that where Arthur Thompson's heading?*

It was vital that they caught him before he got to the river. If he jumped in, the strong tide would quickly carry him away. He would most likely lose his life but he would also escape justice.

Augusta turned the corner onto Bridge Street. There was no sign of Arthur or the police but she jogged toward the river all the same, breathless with exertion. She paused beneath the shadow of Big Ben.

Where have they gone?

A set of steps leading down to a subway caught her eye. She ran down them, hoping Arthur had run that way. The steps levelled out into a tunnel beneath the road along the river embankment.

Where does the tunnel lead?

Augusta ran out into the sunshine and found herself beside Westminster Pier. A steamboat had stopped there and the passengers appeared to have been distracted by a scuffle. Several officers in blue uniforms were grappling with a man who looked as though he had just tried to throw himself into the river.

A short moment later, he appeared to have been subdued.

They had caught him at last.

Chapter 41

"WHAT A LOT OF TEA CHESTS," commented Philip as he surveyed Augusta's workshop. "You've been busy."

"Almost everything's packed away now. You must come and visit my new premises once I've moved in."

"I'd like that."

Augusta glanced around the dingy room. "To think that Arthur Thompson was hiding in here with a knife! Such a horrible thought." She shuddered. "I really couldn't face working down here a moment longer."

"I don't blame you. I take it the new workshop will have a little more light?"

"A lot more. I'm looking forward to setting up the shop as well. I've quite a collection of books to sell already."

"I'm sure you'll do very well with it. Bit of a shame, though."

"Why?"

"Because it means you'll be too busy to help me next time I need a hand."

"I'm sure you won't be needing my help again. You've all the men you could want at the Yard."

"But I don't have a lady with your unique skills."

"I don't know about that." Embarrassed by the compliment, Augusta felt keen to move the conversation along. "Anyway, it's good news about Edward Somerville."

"Yes, it was a good prediction of mine that he'd turn up at the hospital in Gerrard's Cross, wasn't it? I suppose he and Mary Daly were hoping to get their stories straight about the burglary at Miss Mortimer's home. I'm pleased he's under arrest again. A lesser charge this time, but burglary is still a serious matter."

"Did he seem very upset about the death of his wife?"

"It's difficult to tell with him, but I should imagine he is."

Augusta thought about Jacqueline Somerville. It was an awful shame that the embittered woman had tried to benefit financially from what she had seen rather than helping with the police investigation.

"I've read the letters she sent Mr Thompson," continued Philip. "They must have made him quite fearful that he'd be found out. In his eyes, he'd already got away with murder once, so he decided to try his luck again."

"He murdered his employer to avoid the shame and disgrace of being exposed as a thief," added Augusta, "and he committed the second murder to cover up the first."

"The man's a coward."

"And he knew it. He admitted it to me, and I responded with a vague platitude. Perhaps I should have paid his comment a little more heed."

"Well, you got him in the end, Augusta."

"What about Edward Somerville and the Stella Marshall case?"

"The recent investigations we've carried out uncovered several similar attacks on young women in the Enfield area about seven years ago. It seems there was a prowler in the area for a while. Fortunately, none of the other women lost their lives like poor Miss Marshall. We'll be undertaking further interviews in the hope that they might give us a better description of the man. Mr Somerville may be off the hook for that particular crime, but we'll have to wait and see what the investigations yield."

"He's certainly been involved in some questionable scenarios."

"He has." Philip nodded. "Both he and Mr Jeffreys were clients of Miss Mortimer, and Miss Daly appears to have been in her employ in her younger years. They were all keen to keep that information hushed up. We'll learn more about that during Mr Somerville's burglary trial, I suppose. He'll struggle to get his own newspaper up and running now, won't he?"

"Yes, I imagine so. Mr Thompson's trial will be an interesting one, too."

"It will, won't it? Let's hope the jury doesn't fall for any of his lies."

"Perhaps he'll quote Shakespeare while he's on the stand!"

"I wouldn't put it past him." Philip checked his watch. "Should we leave now?"

"Oh, yes. We wouldn't want to keep Lady Hereford waiting."

As they left the basement, Augusta took great care to ensure that the door was locked behind her.

"Middlesex Hospital is only about five minutes' walk from here," she said as they headed in the direction of Russell Square.

"I'm still not sure why Lady Hereford wants to meet me so badly."

"She's very keen to meet a detective from Scotland Yard. She told me she's never met one before. And that's quite something, because Lady Hereford has met a lot of people."

～

"So *you're* the dashing inspector," said Lady Hereford from her bed as Augusta and Philip entered the room. "Oh dear," she added. "I see that you rely on a walking stick."

"Indeed I do, Lady Hereford. Perhaps not so dashing after all! It's a pleasure to meet you."

"And a pleasure to meet you, too." The old lady scrutinised him for a moment. "You remind me of my first husband."

"Is that a good thing?" he asked.

"Not entirely good." She turned to Augusta. "But I approve."

"Approve of what, exactly?" Augusta replied.

"I approve of you working with this man. I can't say anything more than that, can I? He's married, and he has a son and dachshund."

"You already seem to know quite a bit about me, Lady Hereford."

"Oh, yes. Augusta talks about you all the time."

"That's not true!" protested Augusta.

"Is it not?" responded Philip. "Now I feel a little disappointed."

Lady Hereford laughed. "Sit down, you two. I want to hear all about your latest adventure. It's terribly boring sitting about in bed all day, you know. Have you caught that airship murderer yet?"

The End

Historical Note

The inspiration for this story came from an article I read in the *British Newspaper Archive*. Titled *To Ascot by Airship*, it was published in *The Scotsman* on 14th June 1921 and was an account by a news reporter of a trip on the *R36* airship organised by the Air Ministry. The purpose of the journey was to promote the possibilities of commercial airship travel while also conducting traffic control duty over Ascot where races were taking place at the famous racecourse there.

The airship lifted off from Pulham Airship Station in Norfolk at 7.30 am and travelled south to London before flying a short distance west to Ascot in Berkshire to carry out traffic control duty. Two 'observers' from Scotland Yard were on board to communicate via radio any block- ages in the traffic. Apparently on this day the traffic was quiet.

The airship then travelled to Croydon Aerodrome, just south of London, where the news reporters' dispatches were dropped by parachute. The airship returned safely to its mast at 10 pm.

The *R36* airship was originally intended as a patrol airship for the Royal Navy during the First World War, but construction wasn't completed until 1921 so the airship was adapted for possible commercial travel with a passenger compartment capable of carrying 50 passengers. A week after the Ascot trip, the *R36* was damaged during landing and put into storage for repairs. The repairs were delayed by the *R38* disaster in August 1921 and the *R36* was eventually refurbished in 1925 with the aim of being used in commercial flights to Egypt. The airship was scrapped the following year once it was recognised it was incapable of safely carrying the amount of fuel needed for travelling to Egypt.

The *R38* airship disaster led to a review of the airship programme. 44 people tragically died on 24th August 1921 when the airship suffered a structural failure over Hull in the north-east of England. The airship crashed into the Humber Estuary and, miraculously, five crew members survived.

I've been imaginative with the timeframe for *Murder in the Air* because Augusta's airship trip takes place in the autumn of 1921 – this was necessary to follow on from the last book! In reality, the trip wouldn't have taken place after the *R38* disaster in August of that year.

Arthur Thompson was justified in being nervous about airship flight. There were several airship accidents in Europe and America during the First World War. Notable accidents after the war include the *R36* in 1921 (44 killed), *Roma* in 1922 (Virginia, USA, 34 killed), *Dixmude* in 1923 (Sicily, Italy, 50 killed), *R101* in 1930 (France, 48 killed), *USS Akron* in 1933 (New Jersey, USA, 73 dead) and –

possibly the most famous because the incident was caught on film – the *LZ 129 Hindenburg* in 1937 (New Jersey, USA, 36 dead, 62 survivors). By the time of the *Hindenburg* disaster, aeroplanes had shorter travel times than airships. That, coupled with the horrific images of the *Hindenburg* fireball, secured the future of planes as the preferred mode of airborne travel.

Pulham Airship Station – known as RNAS Pulham in its day (RNAS stands for Royal Navy Air Service) was a First World War airship station near the village of Pulham St Mary in Norfolk, at its height around 3,000 people were stationed here. The role of the airships at Pulham was to patrol the North Sea searching for German U-boats. Before long, local people nicknamed the airships 'Pulham Pigs'. After the First World War, the airfield remained in operation under the Royal Air Force (RAF) before being closed down in 1958. The site is now farmland and practically nothing of the former air station remains.

Thank you

~

Thank you for reading *Murder in the Air* I really hope you enjoyed it!

Would you like to know when I release new books? Here are some ways to stay updated:

- Like my Facebook page: facebook.com/emilyorganwriter
- Follow me on Goodreads: goodreads.com/emily_organ
- Follow me on BookBub: bookbub.com/authors/emily-organ
- View my other books here: emilyorgan.com

Thank you

And if you have a moment, I would be very grateful if you would leave a quick review of *Murder in the Air* online. Honest reviews of my books help other readers discover them too!

The Penny Green Series

Also by Emily Organ. Escape to 1880s London! A page-turning historical mystery series.

As one of the first female reporters on 1880s Fleet Street, plucky Penny Green has her work cut out. Whether it's investigating the mysterious death of a friend or reporting on a serial killer in the slums, Penny must rely on her wits and determination to discover the truth.

Fortunately she can rely on the help of Inspector James Blakely of Scotland Yard, but will their relationship remain professional?

Find out more here: emilyorgan.com/penny-green-victorian-mystery-series

The Churchill & Pemberley
Series

Also by Emily Organ. Join senior sleuths Churchill and Pemberley as they tackle cake and crime in an English village.

Growing bored in the autumn of her years, Londoner Annabel Churchill buys a private detective agency in a Dorset village. The purchase brings with it the eccentric Doris Pemberley and the two ladies are soon solving mysteries and chasing down miscreants in sleepy Compton Poppleford.

Plenty of characters are out to scupper their chances, among them grumpy Inspector Mappin. Another challenge is their four-legged friend who means well but has a problem with discipline.

But the biggest challenge is one which threatens to derail every case they work on: will there be enough tea and cake?

Find out more here: emilyorgan.com/the-churchill-pemberley-cozy-mystery-series

Made in United States
Troutdale, OR
01/24/2024

17109993R00152